45

A CANDLELIGHT ROMANCE

D1089715

CANDLELIGHT ROMANCES

COUNTERFEIT HONEYMOON

JULIA ANDERS

A CANDLELIGHT ROMANCE

Published by
Dell Publishing Co., Inc.
1 Dag Hammarskjold Plaza
New York, New York 10017

Dell ® TM 681510, Dell Publishing Co., Inc.

ISBN: 0-440-11138-2

Printed in the United States of America

First printing—December 1980

CHAPTER ONE

"Does anyone in this department speak Italian?"

Lynne Delevan had never intended to become an office typist but despite that fact, or maybe because of it, since she was grimly determined to give value for the salary she needed so desperately, she was concentrating so hard on her work that she didn't hear Mrs. Pringle's words.

Mrs. Pringle repeated over the clatter of typewriters, "I'm requested to ask if anyone in this department speaks Italian."

The second time the words penetrated Lynne's consciousness. She looked up. "I speak Italian."

Mrs. Pringle spoke into the phone for a moment, then stood up and said to Lynne, "Come with me, please."

Lynne laid her work aside and followed her department head out of the room. She supposed that a letter needed translating or something of the sort, though as far as she knew the Corey Company was a strictly British firm and didn't deal in imports or exports. Still, Lynne had been working here for only six months and was a very small cog on the wheel, so there was no reason to suppose she knew even a fraction of what went on.

As they walked toward the lift, Mrs. Pringle seemed to be casting a critical eye over Lynne, for all the world, Lynne thought indignantly, as if she were checking to see if my hem is the right length or if I have a button missing.

The lift door swished closed. "You are wanted in the Upper Office," Mrs. Pringle announced.

Lynne's blue eyes widened. No wonder Mrs. Pringle had been giving her such an odd look. None of the underlings ever had business up on the top story, where the executive offices were. Only the company president, Jason Corey, his directors, and a handful of their sleek, superefficient secretaries ever went up to the Upper Office, where according to the jokes bandied about below, even angels feared to tread.

They passed through an outer reception office into an antechamber. Behind a desk with a wooden nameplate bearing the name "Madelaine Cheney" sat one of the most elegant creatures Lynne had ever seen in a business office. Her short auburn hair was a perfectly sculptured coif. Her frock was deceptively simple. Her pale complexion glowed with a pearly translucence. She could have been anywhere from thirty to fifty.

"This is Miss Delevan," Mrs. Pringle said in a hushed tone.

Madelaine Cheney glanced down at a paper on her desk. "Lynne Delevan. Typing pool." Her voice was clear and her words concise. "Come with me, please. Mr. Corey will see you." She nodded a brisk dismissal to Mrs. Pringle as Lynne gasped.

Mr. Corey will see you. Why on earth would Jason Corey want to see anyone personally about an Italian translation?

Miss Cheney touched a button; Lynne could hear a low buzz from what she thought of as the Inner Sanctum, and then the door swung open.

Jason Corey was seated at a desk with windows behind him so that she could not see him clearly at first.

"This is Miss Delevan," Miss Cheney announced.

6

He rose. "Ah, yes, the lady who is going to help us."

Somehow Lynne's mind suddenly went into a turmoil. She had been braced to meet an ogre, but at that moment he seemed so much less a forbidding personage than she expected that she felt almost giddy. He had risen to greet her, which after all was only common courtesy, but somehow she had pictured him as being more lordly and imperious, sitting while his subjects stood. Then, too, there seemed to be a note of genuine warmth in his voice, which made him seem more human.

Miss Cheney unobtrusively guided her forward and then she could see his face. Previously she had only caught a glimpse of him from a distance, striding purposefully out of the building to a waiting car. Now she thought he looked younger than she had imagined, surely not more than thirty-five, perhaps less. He had a thin, aristocratic nose, and lips shaped in a curve that might have labeled him too handsome had they not been so firm and determined. His shoulders were not especially broad under the perfectly tailored suit, but they gave an impression of great strength.

His hooded gray eyes caught her attention. Then, as she took another step forward, she could see lines on his face that made him seem less young, worry lines around the eyes and mouth, and yet they were not deeply etched, only shadowy lines, as if from recent, transitory troubles.

"I understand you speak fluent Italian."

"Si, Signore." She began a flood of words in demonstration.

He held up a commanding hand to stop her and immediately the impression of warmth and courtesy vanished. "That's hardly necessary," he said. "If I

7

understood the language, I wouldn't need you, would I?"

She felt an angry flush on her cheeks. She had been right earlier. *Imperious* was the word for him.

"You scarcely look Italian with that ash-blond hair," he said. He managed to make it sound like an accusation.

Annoyance made her abandon caution. "Many women bleach their hair, Mr. Corey," she said coolly. "Also there are many blond Italians. However, as it happens I am English, and this is my natural color. I have studied Italian for many years."

His eyebrows rose, whether in annoyance at her impertinence or surprise that a lowly office girl would have studied Italian, she could not tell.

"I assume you will be available for overtime work—at suitable recompense?"

The words formed a question, but his tone made it an order. She would have liked to refuse, but there was the hateful burden of her debt to Uncle Simon to consider. Yes, she would be available for overtime work, whether she liked the idea of kowtowing to this martinet or not.

"Where do you live?" he asked abruptly.

"In Kensal Green."

He scowled. "That's the wrong end of London."

His scowl reminded her of old Maestro Bertelli and the reminder set up an automatic inward quaking. The wrong side of London! How dare he? And then, because she hated herself for allowing him to make her tremble inside in fear of criticism, she said recklessly, "Well, I really wanted a house in Mayfair, but I'll have to wait till I get a rise in salary. I'm about a pound a week short of being able to afford the house I had my eye on."

Miss Cheney would never do anything so uninhibited as to gasp, but, standing next to her, Lynne perceived that she was exuding waves of disapproval.

Jason Corey ignored her sarcasm, just as if she hadn't spoken. "It will be quicker if my driver drops you at Harrods to pick up what you need—a change of costume, a dinner dress, night things. Don't take longer than thirty minutes. Johnson will be needed elsewhere today. Miss Cheney will give you a cheque." He paused. "Perhaps it would be better if you went with her and took a taxi back, Maddy."

Lynne was standing speechless, so dumbfounded that words would not come. Clothes! Night things! What did he think she was? She would give him a good piece of her mind!

He was already back at the work on his desk. Of all the infuriating creatures. To make such a suggestion—not even a suggestion, almost a command—and then calmly dismiss her as if he never so much as questioned her answer.

She opened her mouth to speak, but the efficient Miss Cheney was smoothly pulling her out of the room. The door closed silently behind them, and Lynne turned furiously to the older woman, only to see that she had pushed a button on her intercom and was speaking into it. "Have Johnson bring Mr. Corey's car at once, please," she said crisply. To Lynne, as she took her purse out of a drawer, she said, "Come along."

"Miss Cheney," Lynne sputtered, "I don't know what this is all about or why you and Mr. Corey should imagine I'm going anywhere in his car where I'll need night clothes, but I can tell you—"

"Keep your voice down," Miss Cheney said authoritatively as they crossed the reception room. When they were in the lift, she turned to face Lynne. "You are going to Longridge, Mr. Corey's house in the country, where you will try to provide some assistance in his behalf. If it has crossed your mind that he has designs on your virtue, all I can tell you is that you are behaving like a foolish child who's been seeing too many cheap films. Now pick up your purse and coat, but don't stop to chat."

Somehow Lynne found herself swept out of the building and into a black limousine that was drawn up to the curb. Miss Cheney gave an order to the driver, and the car moved out into the flow of traffic.

Lynne took a deep breath and turned to her companion. "Now, would it be too much to ask what this is all about?"

"As I told you, you are to go to Longbridge, where you will remain for several days—as long as you are needed. Mr. Corey is leaving for Scotland this afternoon. His nephew, who speaks no English, is staying at Longridge. It is with regard to his nephew that your fluency in Italian is expected to be of service."

Lynne's eyes grew wide. She had allowed herself to be calmed by Miss Cheney's words in the lift, almost ashamed of having imagined there was anything wrong with Jason Corey's insistence that she go to his home for an indefinite stay. She had been trying to tell herself that she was just, as Miss Cheney had said, being a foolish girl. But this was even worse. Expected to be of service in regard to his nephew!

"What do you think I am? A common call girl?" she asked with quiet fury.

Miss Cheney turned contemptuous eyes on her. "No, I think you are an extremely tiresome, nonsensical child with exaggerated notions of your own charm. Oh, I'll grant that you have a lovely complexion, fine eyes, and a mouth that could be pretty if you weren't always pulling it into absurd expressions of indignation. But do you honestly think so highly of yourself as to imagine that a man like Mr. Corey would raid the typing pool for female companionship—for himself or his nephew?"

Lynne suddenly felt terribly gauche. She knew she was blushing madly. "But—" she began.

"In point of fact, Mr. Corey has interests elsewhere. And his nephew is five years old."

Lynne subsided completely, feeling very small. "If you'd only explained—"

"If you'd only come down off your high ropes long enough to let me. Surely you are aware that Mr. Corey's brother was killed in a car crash three weeks ago. I'm sure it must have been downstairs gossip at the time."

Lynne frowned, shaking her head. "I hadn't heard. I was ill with flu and missed a week's work about that time. I'm sorry."

"Morgan Corey lived in Turin with his Italian wife. They were on holiday in Spain with their son when the crash occurred. Morgan was killed instantly, his wife critically injured. Mr. Corey went to Spain to bring his brother's body home for burial. The wife was in a hospital in Madrid, too ill to be moved. Her parents were on a world cruise somewhere in the South Pacific and couldn't get back immediately, so Mr. Corey brought his nephew back to Longridge.

"The problem is that Mr. Corey's nephew is turning the house upside down. He won't eat; he cries all the time. Now the cook is threatening to quit. Mr. Corey's domestic tranquility is being seriously threatened."

"The poor child," Lynne murmured. "Who can blame him for crying? His father and mother suddenly vanished. And only five years old. Hasn't it occurred to anyone that it's natural for him to be upset?"

"Of course it has, but no one can communicate with him and no one can cope."

"And that's where I come in," Lynne said.

Miss Cheney nodded. "It's a pity he didn't learn English, but Morgan wanted to improve his Italian so they always used that language at home. Since they were in a lively social set, the child spent much of his time with a nursemaid who spoke no English."

The car drew up to Harrods. "We'll try to make this brief, Johnson," she said. "Mr. Corey said half an hour, but I think we might stretch it to forty-five minutes."

Lynne could understand why Miss Cheney was a good executive secretary. Without a wasted word or motion, she had Lynne in a dressing room with a saleswoman bringing dinner dresses for her to try on and two others dispatched to search out nightwear, underclothes, and a skirt and sweater set.

"Something conservative," she had said.

The navy blue crepe slid over her head and Lynne regarded herself in the mirror. It was a nicer dress than she'd ever owned. Not exciting, perhaps, but the expensive cut seemed to bring elegance to her slender figure.

"That should do," Miss Cheney decided.

"If I might be permitted," the saleswoman said, having returned with another dress. "Perhaps this might suit the young lady's coloring better."

Miss Cheney was about to refuse but the skirts had not arrived yet, and Lynne had given such an audible gasp of pleasure when she saw the delectable shade of periwinkle blue, that she changed her mind and nodded. "Go ahead. Try it."

Lynne couldn't believe the image in the mirror. She had never worn anything so lovely in her life. It was cut along the lines of the robes worn by medieval princesses, close-fitting through the midsection, showing off Lynne's trim waist, and then cleverly flaring in soft folds. The sleeves were long; it was a perfectly proper dress, and yet somehow beautifully romantic.

"You can see what the color does for her eyes," the saleswoman said, "and if she would wear her hair loose, like this—" She released two of the pins at the sides and the ash-blond hair tumbled softly around Lynne's face.

A series of expressions crossed Miss Cheney's usually controlled face—surprise, speculation, and finally a kind of wry amusement. "We'll take that one," she decided.

Lynne gasped. "But I couldn't. It must be terribly expensive. Besides, I don't understand why I even need a dinner dress to be a sort of baby-sitter."

"Who knows what may turn up?" Miss Cheney said enigmatically. "Mr. Corey won't be in Scotland long. It's possible that dinnertime will be the only chance he has to talk to you about his nephew. Perhaps he'll have guests and need you to make an even number at table." Her look of slightly malicious amusement was back, though Lynne couldn't understand why. "Just remember, anything's possible, and you must be prepared. And he did specify a dinner dress."

When the other clothes were brought, she quickly chose a skirt and sweater set in a clear coral and a daytime frock of pale gold-beige, almost the color of Lynne's hair. The plain brown robe and underthings she simply agreed to as they were brought, without giving Lynne a chance to try them on, asking that everything be wrapped and delivered to the front entrance immediately.

"Evening slippers, and that should do it," she said. "Come along; don't dawdle."

"Dawdle?" Lynne said in amazement. "It usually takes me longer than this to choose a new blouse."

"Ah, but the difference is that today we don't have longer to spend. When a decision must be made quickly, you'll find it usually can be done."

The car was waiting when they reached the entrance. Madelaine Cheney leaned into the car and put something into Lynne's hand. "This is just a little personal gift from me. For luck."

Before Lynne even had time to stammer out a surprised thank you, she had slammed the door and the car was moving.

She opened the package to find a small atomizer bottle of perfume. What an unexpected thing for the cool, efficient Miss Cheney to have done!

Lynne leaned back and closed her eyes. This had certainly been one of the most confusing days of her life. She hoped she could help the poor child at Long-ridge—Tonio was his name, Miss Cheney had said—but for his own sake, not his hateful uncle's.

It was strange how in that first moment she had warmed to him. He had seemed—just for an instant—charming and very human. And then between one second and the next, he had revealed himself as auto-cratic and dictatorial, ordering her around with no thought whatever for her feelings.

She wondered if he had recognized her outrage and known what her suspicions were. Probably he had and didn't care, not as long as she did as she was told, calmed his nephew, and prevented his cook from leaving. Did he even care about the boy, or was he just concerned that his household continued to run smoothly?

She decided he was probably completely heartless

and she hated him—all the more because of that first minute in which her judgment of him had proven so wrong.

Nevertheless, she would do her best for the little boy.

CHAPTER TWO

As the big car slowed to a crawl, passing through a pretty little village, Lynne leaned forward and asked Johnson how much farther to Longridge.

"About twenty minutes, miss."

Suddenly she had butterflies in her stomach. She sat back and took three deep breaths the way Maestro Bertelli had always told her to do.

It was funny how Jason Corey's scowl had brought Maestro Bertelli back so clearly, and the memory of her inward quaking when she feared she had displeased him. He had always been very strict with her but only because he had wanted her to be the best. He had never doubted that she would be.

She couldn't remember a time when she didn't know she would be a singer. Her parents had told her she sang little tunes before she could talk clearly. One of her earliest remembered joys was of listening to the phonograph records from her father's collection —his one extravagance.

Her dear father—so much older than her mother, but always so gentle and loving. He was a musician, too, an amateur but gifted cellist. He and a group of friends had spent Sunday afternoons playing chamber music for their own pleasure.

Lynne had grown up with the sounds of music around her, and when it became apparent that her voice was special—more than just a sweet voice that her parents, being parents, would naturally take pride in—her father insisted that she have only the best teachers, those who could be trusted to develop her voice without straining it. "This is a delicate instrument, my dear," he had said, touching her throat.

When she was thirteen, he persuaded Bertelli to listen to her. The Maestro immediately agreed to take her on as a pupil. "My child," he told her, "your voice has the soaring beauty of a bird in flight. And that is the last compliment I shall pay you. From now on it is work, and only work. You will often hate me, but together we shall discipline the bird in your throat, and if we both work to the best of our capacity, you will become a great lyric soprano."

Her mother went back to her old job in a library to help pay for Lynne's lessons. Besides her music, she studied languages—French, German, but she worked hardest on Italian, because the Maestro believed that her voice would be best suited for the Italian operas.

Her father did not live long after Bertelli began her training, but he died confident of her future success. He left only a small insurance policy, but with her mother's salary and living with great frugality, they managed.

Then when Lynne was seventeen, her beloved mother was suddenly gone. Lynne was devastated. Since her father had died, the only two important things in her life were her mother and her music. She had no family other than one querulous uncle, her mother's older brother. She had never had time for close friendships and the casual pleasures of youth because there was always her work, study and practicing, to be done. Now she had only her music.

Bertelli took charge. He found an older pupil willing to share her flat with Lynne. He found money for a scholarship. He kept her too busy to give her undue time to grieve.

For months she went through the motions of work like an automaton, but then the discipline of a lifetime took over and she was working in earnest again and her deep love of music asserted itself once more and gave purpose to her days.

Occasionally the Maestro allowed his students to sing in public, but only what he felt their voices were properly prepared for and always under his personal direction.

In March of the year she had turned nineteen, Bertelli was invited to direct a production of *Lucia di Lammermoor* at the University of Leeds. He assigned Lynne the role of Lucia.

She had never been so happy with her work, preparing for the role, rehearsing her part, traveling to Leeds. She had a few moments of nervousness before her entrance, but once on stage pouring forth Lucia's lovely liquid sounds, she felt as if she was where she belonged.

The audience loved it. Even the Maestro smiled and said, "Well done," which from him amounted to an accolade.

The troupe was very gay on the bus trip home. A late snow, followed by sleet, had turned the countryside to a crystal fairyland. Much as she loved the green lushness of summer, Lynne thought she had never seen anything so lovely as the silent white landscape from the bus window as it flashed by, the trees mantled in pearl, glistening here and there with a diamond brilliance.

That was the last thing she remembered before the crash on the bridge.

She woke in a hospital, her head and neck swathed in bandages. Quiet, reassuring voices spoke to her; efficient hands cared for her. Only half awake in the days that followed, she was aware of an intravenous tube in her arm, but she could move all her limbs. Then the bandages were removed from her eyes, and she could see, so she knew she was basically all right. Day by day the pain subsided and eventually the doctor came in and removed the rest of the bandages.

"Now we can get rid of the tube and you can eat some real food for a change—some of our delicious hospital food," he said, smiling.

With one hand she touched her face. She could feel no scars. "Am I all right?" she whispered.

"Your face is perfect," he said, and then abruptly left.

The first tray of food might not have been haute cuisine, but it tasted delicious. It was not until she tried to thank the attendant who came to take away her tray that she realized her voice was coming out in a whisper again.

Sudden fear paralyzed her. "Why can't I talk?" she croaked agonizingly.

"Just rest," she was told. "Give your body a chance to heal."

She did as she was told. She rested. She tried not to panic. She began to improve. She could talk hoarsely, no longer in that terrible whisper. She was examined and reexamined. There was no cause for the lump of fear inside her, she told herself. She was getting better. She would continue to improve until she was back to normal. Then with work and careful exercise, the instrument, the delicate instrument that was her voice, would be retuned.

Bertelli himself came to see her, not once but many times. He took her home to London to her little flat. Weeks went by and she could talk fairly normally, but still with a husky quality to her voice, not clear, liquid sounds as before. Cautiously she tried to vocalize. In the middle range the tones were harsh. The high notes she couldn't hit at all.

Bertelli took her to private specialists. Then one sunny day in June the final verdict was in. The laryngeal nerves had suffered permanent damage from the blow to her neck. No further improvement could be expected.

She was very lucky, they told her, that she could speak so normally. Her speaking voice had a very interesting, pleasing quality, they told her. It could have been much worse. Yes, they agreed; she was very lucky.

She walked out of the doctor's office and sat shivering in the warm sun.

The bird in her throat was stilled forever. She would never sing again.

She felt as if her whole life had been a dream, her aspirations only fantastic and beautiful shapes carved in ice. Then the sun had come out and the ice had melted; her dreams had melted away like water which seeped into the ground and vanished.

Madame Bertelli came to see her. "I know you think life is over," she said, "but you are wrong. Life offers many paths. Sometimes the one we choose is blocked. Then we have to turn and try a different route. You are very young, little Lynne. It may take a long time but you will find your path. Once I wanted to be a violinist, but I lacked that divine spark, so now I enjoy music, but as a listener. Instead of making music, I fell in love with Bertelli, married him, raised his children. It is hard to believe I could have been happier as a concert violinist. My best wish for you is that you have as happy a life as I, and remember, the first path I chose was blocked, too. Nothing is ever wasted. Perhaps something you have learned in your striving will point the way to your new path."

She had to find a way to live. She was prepared for nothing but singing. She knew languages, but she had not attended a university and she had no teaching credentials. She thought of becoming a tutor, but no one wanted a young English girl as an Italian tutor when there were plenty of genuine Italians around.

Her mother's brother Simon, as Lynne's next of kin, had been notified of her accident. He had written her a brief note saying he hoped she would soon recover, which she supposed was as near to expressing sympathy as he ever allowed himself. How such an irritable, dried-up character could be related to her outgoing, warm mother, Lynne couldn't imagine, though of course he was only a half-brother. He had had an unfortunate marriage, and he was plagued with attacks of arthritis. Perhaps these things had warped his character.

When Lynne was at lowest ebb, working as a counter girl in a rather unpleasant café, trying to make ends meet, her Uncle Simon appeared in London, down from Manchester on business.

"Well, you've really got yourself in a fine mess, haven't you?" he demanded. "I never did hold with that la-di-da, impractical training your parents gave you. All that time and money down the drain, and what's to show for it? What, I ask you?" His small black eyes glittered at her maliciously.

"Please, Uncle Simon." There were tears in Lynne's own eyes. "There's no use trying to change what's past."

"I'll tell you what I propose," he said. "Not that I believe in bailing out people too improvident to avoid going out in a leaky boat, but you're my sister's only chick. I'll stake you to a business course. Pay for your training and living expenses. As soon as you get a job, you can start paying me back."

"But, Uncle," Lynne protested, "though it's very kind of you, I haven't the least inclination for secretarial work."

"Well, do you have an inclination for starving?" he barked. "Or wiping greasy counters in a café?"

"I'd thought of teaching languages," she faltered. "If I could get my qualification—"

"More folderol!" he interrupted. "The English language is good enough for anyone. You learn to type and keep accounts—you won't starve."

At last she had given in because there was really no other way out. Though she tried to be grateful, he had said so many insulting things about the impracticality of her parents that she knew she could never forgive him.

She would take the course he insisted upon and live frugally—hanging on until the debt was paid—and then somehow, working nights and studying days, she would find a way to qualify as a teacher.

She had found it harder to repay the debt than she had dreamed. She lived simply, allowing herself no luxuries, and every week she sent a small amount to him on account, but the outstanding debt still loomed impossibly large, and in the meantime she was stuck in a job she cordially disliked.

Until today. Confused as her feelings were, at least today she was having a holiday from her beastly typewriter. Surely Jason Corey had meant what he had said about "suitable recompense for overtime." That should allow her to wipe out a larger portion of the debt than she was usually able to do in a week.

Meanwhile, she would try to forget having made an idiot of herself over suspecting him of dishonorable intentions, and enjoy the sensation of riding in a beautiful car with the loveliest collection of clothes she'd ever owned in her life stowed in the boot.

At the thought of the clothes, a pang smote her. He couldn't, surely, be intending to subtract the cost of the clothes from her wages, could he? Because if so, even with the overtime, it would take a year to pay for them, and there was the money for Uncle Simon owing, too. Her thoughts chased themselves around and around.

"Take three deep breaths and calm down," she told herself. It helped, because then she thought of Miss Cheney. Even if Jason Corey, in his lordly arrogance, had no notion what she earned and deemed it only fitting that she should be prepared to outfit herself properly to cross his threshold, she had no doubt that Miss Cheney could gauge very accurately what her salary was and she would never have insisted on such expensive things—that heavenly blue dinner dress, for instance—if she had been expected to pay for them herself.

Miss Cheney wouldn't have put her in such a position, she was sure, because even though she'd called her a tiresome little fool at first, later she'd been quite nice—as if she were on Lynne's side—even giving her that little flacon of perfume.

Of course she would give the clothes back when her time at Longridge was over. A sudden giggle rose to her lips as she wondered what Jason Corey would do with them.

Then her smile faded as she remembered how he had thought better of giving her a cheque and asked Miss Cheney to go along and choose her outfits. She supposed he didn't trust her to have decent taste. Well, he was wrong about that. She had studied costuming and she knew what became her, but knowing wasn't much help if you couldn't afford anything new and attractive.

"Here's the house, miss." Johnson's words broke in upon her thoughts. She peered out. The car had turned up a long lane of trees. At the end all she could see was red brick, a soft glowing rose-red with touches of white. Then they swept onto a circular drive and the whole of the house was revealed.

It was not a huge house but it was gracefully proportioned, and in the circle of the drive a profusion of flowers grew, not in the neatly trimmed beds that Lynne always felt looked so stiff and touch-me-not, but massed in a riot of color.

Before she was out of the car, the door of the house opened and a tall woman in black stepped out to greet her. If Lynne hadn't been so nervous, she would have felt very grand mounting the steps.

"Miss Delevan? We've been expecting you. I'm Mrs. Edgers, the housekeeper." There was a young, rosy-faced maid hovering in the background. "I'll show you to your room," Mrs. Edgers went on, "and Hatton will unpack for you."

Lynne decided there was no way to be grand when her luggage consisted of nothing but parcels, so she might as well tell the simple truth. "I'm afraid I live in the wrong end of London, Mrs. Edgers. Mr. Corey decided that Johnson couldn't be spared long enough to take me so far in that direction to pack, so instead we stopped and picked up some new things to tide me over for a few days. Of course I travel to work by Underground and it doesn't take nearly as long as it does driving through traffic."

As they walked along the upper hallway, much as she would have liked to explore her room in this beautiful house, Lynne said, "I won't stop in my

25

room now. I'd like to see Tonio immediately, if that's possible."

Mrs. Edgers's lips compressed at the mention of his name. "Certainly, miss." She opened a door and Lynne could see her room, pale yellow with touches of a rich, deep blue. "Hatton, take Miss Delevan along to Master Tonio's room now. You can come back directly and unpack."

"Hatton, tell me about Tonio," Lynne said after the little maid had deposited her parcels in the yellow room and Mrs. Edgers had left them. "I can understand that he's grief-stricken and lonely, and it must be terribly frustrating not being able to talk to anyone, but what does he do that's upsetting the household so much?"

"Acts up something fierce, he does, miss," Hatton said, her eyes round. "Yells and takes on dreadful, all in that heathen tongue so nobody can tell what he wants. Screams when he has to go to bed and won't eat hardly nothing. Mrs. Baggett, she's the cook, tries ever such nourishing food, he's that thin, miss, but he won't have none of it. Getting worse, too, he is. Lately a couple of times he's thrown his food on the floor. Mrs. Baggett's threatening to give notice and Mrs. Edgers isn't half upset. Mrs. Baggett suits the Master fine and she won't be easy to replace."

She threw open the door of a pleasantly light room, and there by the window, arms on the sill, head buried in his arms, crouched a small boy.

So this was the monster who was turning the house upside down, Lynne thought wryly.

"Master Tonio, you have a visitor," Hatton said.

At the sound of her voice, he lifted his head and turned around. His eyes were enormous, dark pools of despair.

Lynne's heart turned over. "*Ciao*, Tonio." Speaking in clear Italian she said, "I'm Lynne. I've come to talk to you and be your friend. We have so much to talk about. Could we begin being each other's friend now? *Immediatamente?*"

She held out her arms and he hurtled into them, burying his face in her skirt.

CHAPTER THREE

It was Friday afternoon three days later and Lynne was playing a rowdy game of catch with Tonio down near the woods behind the house. She was wearing her old clothes, for fear of soiling the new skirt, and a good thing, too, she thought, as she crawled under a bush to retrieve a wild pitch of Tonio's.

"Attenzione! Non faccia così!" she called to him.

"Well, I wouldn't know about that," a masculine voice answered, and she looked up to see Jason Corey standing there in impeccable tweeds with a faintly amused look on his face.

Smug and *superior* were the words that came to her mind as she scrambled to her feet, humiliated at being caught in such a position. She brushed the leaves from her skirt, calling in Italian to Tonio, "Come and say good afternoon to your uncle."

Jason Corey bent down and gave the boy a stiff little hug, to which Tonio submitted. "Well, old boy, you're looking better." To Lynne, he said, "Things are progressing. Last time I came to see him he took one look at me and burst into tears."

"Is it to be wondered at? You're the one who brought him here away from everything and everyone he knows. Is there any news of his mother?"

"I called the hospital in Madrid this morning. There's no change. She still isn't conscious."

"Oh, dear," Lynne said, trying to keep the dismay out of her voice. "That sounds very bad, doesn't it?"

Tonio was clutching at her skirt, asking for news of his mother. "Your uncle called the hospital today. The doctors and nurses are all working very hard to help her."

Hatton appeared, breathless, from the direction of the house. "Mrs. Edgers says to tell you there's a call from London," she announced.

He nodded. "I want to talk to you about the boy, but I've some business to attend to. We'll have our discussion at dinner."

"I'm sorry," she said, "but there's a shop in the village that serves pizza. I've promised Tonio to take him there to eat tonight."

"You can do that another time," he said, as if it were of no consequence.

"I'm afraid not," she said stubbornly. "Tonio trusts me. I gave him my word. I think it would be very harmful if I broke my promise. He has been behaving very politely to the cook and housekeeper for two days to earn this treat."

Tonio spoke to her, looking from her to his uncle.

"What did he say?" Jason demanded.

Lynne bit her lip.

"Well, come on, out with it."

"He wants me to ask if you would like to come to supper with us," she said reluctantly, hoping he wouldn't think it was her idea to invite him.

"And upset Mrs. Baggett again when she's prepared my dinner?" he asked coldly. "No, thank you. Perhaps you'll have the goodness to join me when you've finished your expedition. I presume that at his age he dines early."

"Yes, but then I have to read to him before he goes to sleep. That is, I bought some children's storybooks and I translate them as he looks at the pictures."

30

"At your convenience then," he said sarcastically and stalked off.

What arrogance, she thought, coming down here and expecting everyone to jump to his command. Then guiltily she realized he had every right to expect just that. She was his employee, after all. However, her promise to Tonio took precedence over her duty to her employer because the boy's need to trust her was more important than Jason Corey's need to be obeyed.

"My uncle is very handsome, isn't he?" Tonio asked. "He looks much like my father."

"I'm sure your father was a very handsome man," she said, not quite answering his question. "Come along now. It's time for your bath, so you'll be very handsome when we go to dinner."

Jason Corey was having coffee in the library by the time she finished putting Tonio to bed. They had had a jolly evening in the gay little café and he had giggled all the way through his bedtime story and kissed her warmly good night.

She paused on the threshold of the library. What a contrast, she thought, seeing her employer sitting there so stiff and silent. As if he were a little lonely —a little out of it, the thought came to her mind, but she dismissed it as nonsense.

He looked up and saw her standing there in the new coral skirt and sweater outfit and for a moment it almost seemed as if his face brightened. Then he said dryly, "I trust you enjoyed a delicious dinner, Miss Delevan."

"Tonio had fun, I think," she answered defensively.

He gestured her to a chair and poured a cup of coffee for her.

"Well, now." His eyes seemed to pierce her. "Tell me about this magical transformation you've performed on my nephew."

"There isn't any magic. It was just being able to talk the same language. Can't you imagine how terrified he was? His father dead, not knowing where his mother was, not being able to ask anyone. He's so young, and here he was surrounded by grownups who not only couldn't talk to him, but didn't even stop to think that little boys need to play. Even so soon after a loss like the one he had, children need to play."

He nodded. "But he wouldn't even eat. Mrs. Baggett seems to have calmed down, so you must have worked some magic there."

"Not really. It's just that Mrs. Baggett's idea of how to feed a child didn't take into account he is an Italian child. You know how it is when you're away from home and miserable. Familiar food is a comfort. I don't think most children are great experimenters when it comes to eating. Mrs. Baggett kept giving him things she considered great treats, like steak and kidney pudding, and roast mutton, and shepherd's pie, and treacle tarts. He'd never tasted any of them before and was in no mood to try to like anything new. And she kept trying to make him eat porridge for breakfast. And then, when he asked for ice cream, saying *gelato,* of course, she nodded as if she understood and gave him a dish of gelatin. I think that was what he threw on the floor," she admitted.

Jason laughed and it transformed his whole face, easing the stern lines around his mouth.

"So all I really did was ask him what he liked," continued Lynne, "and he's been quite greedily consuming all the veal scallops and pasta and chicken that she fixes.

"Then there was the matter of his not wanting to go to sleep. Well, he was accustomed to a bedtime story, but he always slept with a teddy bear, and it was just the last straw when that was gone, too. Of course I couldn't provide the old one, but we went to the village and chose a new one, and it seems to have helped."

"I'll reimburse you, of course."

"Thank you, but I'd rather not. You see, it was my special gift to him."

He gave her a long, level look.

She flushed. "I suppose you're thinking that I'm being very silly—that as you pay my wages, it's your money anyway. But there's a difference you know, with a gift."

"No, I wasn't thinking that at all. I was thinking that you're a rather unexpected young lady."

There was silence for a moment and then he said, "I'd like you to stay on a bit longer, if that's agreeable. It's obvious you're doing Tonio a world of good."

"Of course I will, if that's what you want." She rose to go.

"And by the way," he added, "don't make any plans with Tonio for dinner tomorrow. Some people are coming for the weekend, and I'll expect you to dine with us."

Her heart skipped a beat, but only because of the new dinner dress, of course. She'd get to wear the beautiful blue dress at least once.

The guests were to arrive at varying times during the afternoon. It was a fine day and Lynne decided it might be more pleasant for Tonio if she took him for a picnic lunch and walk, so he wouldn't have to stay dressed up and on his best behavior for too many hours. She could see that he was cleaned up and presented about teatime if Jason Corey wished him shown to the guests.

Mrs. Baggett was nowhere to be seen when Lynne went to the kitchen; only the young maid, Hatton, who was helping out by cleaning vegetables.

"I'm going to pack a lunch for Tonio and me," Lynne said. "I don't think Mrs. Baggett would mind if I sliced some of this leftover joint for sandwiches, do you?"

"I shouldn't think so, miss," Hatton said. "She wouldn't be serving leftovers to guests. She fusses, Mrs. Baggett does, about having everything just so when there's people staying here. Not that this is much of a party. There's only to be Mr. Lloyd—he does legal work for the Master—and then there's the nice old doctor and his wife, and Mrs. Grant."

"And Mr. Grant?" Lynne asked idly, buttering slices of bread.

"Oh, there is no Mr. Grant, miss," Hatton confided. "Leastways, there is one, but he and Mrs. Grant have been separated quite some time. Now they're divorcing, or trying to. It's all of a tangle because Mrs. Grant inherited some big company from her dad and Mr. Grant runs the company and over the years got a lot of stock, and it's taking time to sort things out. I was clearing up the coffee things one night and I heard Mr. Lloyd tell the Master it would be a miracle if Mrs. Grant was free in less than a year. The Master didn't half look glum at that. I heard Mrs. Baggett and Mrs. Edgers talking, and it seems Mrs. Grant and the Master are expecting to marry after the divorce."

Lynne sliced the sandwiches in two with a vigorous

stroke of the knife. "It seems to me you overhear quite a bit."

"Well, of course, miss," Hatton said, unperturbed. "I will say Mrs. Grant is a fair treat to look at. There's something about the way she looks at things though, you know?"

"No," Lynne said. "I don't know."

"I don't know as I can explain it. It's just a funny feeling I get. When her eyes touch on a thing, it's like she was seeing something different from what I see. Sometimes gives me the shivers, it does."

"You have a fertile imagination," Lynne said, twisting the top on the bottle of milk. "You can tell Mrs. Baggett that I know she's busy today and I'll see to Master Tonio's supper myself."

It was just bad luck that Jason Corey and Mrs. Grant were in the garden when Lynne and Tonio returned from their hike, Lynne in her old clothes, her hair dishevelled.

Hatton was right. Mrs. Grant was a fair treat to look at. She had a perfect oval face and improbably pale hair, almost silver, parted in the center and hanging straight as a length of silk. Lynne wasn't sure if her eyes were really green or if it was just the makeup that made them look that way.

"Justine, I'd like you to meet Miss Delevan and my nephew, Tonio. This is Mrs. Grant."

Lynne translated for Tonio and added that he must step forward and take her hand.

He did so, looking at her carefully, then asked Lynne, "Is she in a circus? There was a clown in a circus I saw with that green stuff around his eyes."

Lynne choked slightly.

"What did the little darling say?" Justine Grant cooed.

"He apologized for his appearance, but we've been on a long ramble," Lynne improvised.

"And he's taken his teddy with him. Such a big boy to carry around a teddy. Let me see it."

She reached for the toy bear he carried under his arm, and like a flash he had jerked it away and stepped behind Lynne for protection.

"Well!" There was chilly amusement in Justine's voice.

"Sorry; that was a special gift from Miss Delevan. He doesn't allow anyone to touch it," Jason intervened.

Justine turned appraising eyes on Lynne for the first time. In that one brief look she seemed to size up her age, the price of her outfit, and probably made an accurate guess as to the amount of her savings. "Ah, yes, you're little Tonio's nurse."

"Temporarily," Lynne said coolly. "If you'll excuse us, I'll take Tonio up and see to his bath."

The dress was as lovely as Lynne remembered, perhaps even lovelier, here in this gracious setting, than it had looked that day when she was so confused and harried and had first seen herself in it in the fitting room mirror.

She arranged her hair to tumble softly around her face as the saleswoman had suggested. She added just a touch of color to her lips and a spray of the perfume that Madelaine Cheney had so unexpectedly pressed into her hand. Her curly lashes were thick and dark, and she had never needed to enhance them with cosmetics.

It was good to know she was looking her very best because there was no doubt she was nervous. "Three breaths and I'll be ready," she told herself.

She went down a little early, thinking perhaps she could be of help to the housekeeper, and also because she felt it was not appropriate for an employee to make a grand entrance.

She found that her employer was ahead of her in the drawing room. He turned and stared at her quite blankly for a moment. Then his high arching brows rose briefly in surprise, but almost immediately his strong features were rearranged in an expression of careful control.

"I thought there might be something I could do to help," she said.

"Nothing, I think." His eyes were still on hers. "Let me pour you a sherry."

She hesitated, but he had already turned to the crystal decanter.

"Tonio behaved very nicely when you brought him to greet the guests at tea time," he said. "You've done wonders."

She shook her head. "He's a very sweet child. He just needs to know what's expected of him. Naturally, I think he's as polite as—well, as a five-year-old boy can be expected to be."

"Unless someone tries to touch his toy bear." He grinned. "Tell me what it was he really said to Mrs. Grant."

She feigned innocence. "I don't know what you mean."

"You translated it as an apology for his appearance, but somehow I think that's a great deal more polite than a five-year-old boy can be expected to be."

She stifled a laugh and fortunately at that moment three of the guests appeared on the threshold.

Dr. and Mrs. Bannister were a charming middle-aged couple, who, Lynne gathered, lived somewhere in the vicinity and were not staying in the house for the weekend. Darren Lloyd was another guest down from London, whom Hatton had described as "doing the Master's legal work." He was a large man of about forty with an openness of face that made him seem completely trustworthy.

It was left to Justine, in the end, to make an entrance, and an entrance it was. She was dressed all in pale, shimmering gold with jewelry at her wrists and throat.

Jason crossed immediately to greet her. She looked up at him with a smile, murmuring something too low for the others to catch.

She looked quite breathtaking, Lynne thought, if perhaps a bit overdressed for a country weekend, especially a quiet weekend where the host had lost a member of his family scarcely a month ago. But the two of them made a stunning couple, he so dark and she so fair.

Mrs. Grant turned to greet the others, not so much looking at them as looking for her own reflection in their faces, until she saw Lynne. It was obvious that for an instant she did not recognize her, and then her eyes narrowed, glittering. Lynne read speculation there and no pleasure. Sitting down to the beautiful table with its magnificent flowers, and fine old silver gleaming softly in the candlelight, Lynne felt as if she were in a dream.

She was content merely to let the conversation flow around her as she enjoyed the sensations of being in such a setting. The soup was delicious. Not until midway through the fish course did she really begin to listen to what the others were saying. They were discussing the newest rage of the London stage, arguing over whether he was really, as some critics predicted, a new Olivier.

At her right Dr. Bannister asked, "And what do you think of the fellow, Miss Delevan?"

"I'm afraid I haven't seen him," she said quietly.

"What? Not in either of his plays?" Justine Grant said in mock surprise. "Perhaps Miss Delevan doesn't care for the theatre."

"It isn't a matter of not caring for it, though I do prefer opera," Lynne replied.

"Opera? Then doubtless you have an opinion on that new diva—what's her name? Sophana Arlandi?" There was an undercurrent of malicious amusement in her voice. It was obvious that she supposed Lynne would never have heard Arlandi perform, but Maestro Bertelli frequently saw to it that she was provided with tickets for the opera.

"I think she's long on histrionics and short on technique," Lynne said coolly.

The answer didn't please Justine. "Which roles have you heard her sing?"

Lynne named all three in which Arlandi had appeared.

"I haven't heard her myself," Mrs. Bannister said, "but they do say she has quite a following already."

"I daresay," Lynne replied. "Some people prefer dramatic flair to vocal perfection. And she is a fine actress."

"Are you trying to say she sings flat?" Justine asked contemptuously.

"That wasn't quite what I meant," Lynne said. "Her phrasing is frequently imprecise and her intonation is not always secure. Though in point of fact she did sing flat once in *Bohème*."

"I suppose you have perfect pitch?" Justine said with just a trace of a sneer.

"Yes, I have," Lynne replied, unconcerned.

"How interesting," Darren Lloyd said quickly, drawing attention away from the annoyance that was all too easy to read on Justine's face. He tapped his wine goblet wtih a spoon. "Can you tell what that note was?"

She smiled at him. "An A."

Jason repeated the act with his own glass. "And what about mine?"

"Oh, dear," she said. "I'm afraid your glass is out of tune. That falls somewhere between an F-sharp and a G."

In the laughter that followed, she glanced at Justine Grant and saw that she had made an implacable enemy.

On Sunday Lynne would have liked to beg off from lunch, but Jason told her that he, Darren, and Justine would be leaving for London shortly afterward and she would have the rest of the day to attend to Tonio's needs.

She put on the gold-beige frock and made a resolution not to do anything that would draw attention to herself and further annoy Justine. She needn't have worried. Justine behaved as if she weren't there at all.

Most of the time she talked directly to Jason while Darren courteously chatted with Lynne. Toward the end of lunch, Jason gave her several suggestions for outings in the neighborhood that Tonio might enjoy.

When they had left, the house was very quiet. Lynne took off her finery, put on her old suit, and went for a walk with Tonio.

On Wednesday Jason called from London. His sister-in-law had regained consciousness. Her parents had just called him from Madrid and wanted Tonio brought to the hospital to see her. Johnson was already on the way to Longridge. Lynne was to bring

Tonio directly to the airport, where Jason would meet them and take the boy to Spain.

Lynne packed away her new clothes carefully in tissue, leaving the blue dress till last.

And so, she thought, another few hours and Cinderella will be back at her own hearthside.

CHAPTER FOUR

When Lynne returned to the office the next morning, she found an envelope on her desk bearing the inter-office notation "From the desk of Madelaine Cheney." Inside she found a note clipped to a cheque. "Before Mr. Corey left for Spain, he asked me to give you this cheque in reimbursement for your assistance to his nephew."

She felt a flicker of surprise because she had ex-pected the overtime to be added to her weekly salary cheque, but then she realized that since caring for Tonio had been a personal job for Jason Corey, of course it couldn't come out of company funds.

She unfolded the cheque and looked at it with a sharp intake of breath. It was a good deal more gen-erous than she had expected, and it made her feel guiltier than ever about what had been spent on her clothes.

Before she had time to get cold feet, she made her way to a telephone, dialed the Upper Office, and asked the receptionist if she could be put through to Miss Cheney.

After a moment the crisp voice came on the line with, "Madelaine Cheney here."

"This is Lynne Delevan, Miss Cheney. I wanted to—if this is out of line, please say so and I'll under-stand, but I wondered—" She took a deep breath for courage. "I wondered if I could invite you to lunch."

There was a pause during which Lynne decided she must have committed a terrible faux pas, and then

Miss Cheney was saying, "I've just checked my schedule and I'm free today. Shall we meet in the lower lobby at one?"

When the waiter had taken their order, Lynne said earnestly, "First of all, Miss Cheney, I want to thank you so much for the lovely perfume. It was such a delightful surprise."

"I'm happy you were pleased," the older woman said. "Do you suppose you could call me Madelaine?"

Lynne smiled warmly. "I'd like that. You were so kind to me. Now there is something I'd like to ask you about. The clothes. What should I do with the clothes?"

Madelaine's brows rose. "What do you ordinarily do with clothes? Hang them up? Put them in a drawer?"

"I mean, I wouldn't feel right about keeping them. They cost too much and that cheque was so large—"

"Now, my child. The cheque was not too large. You realize you'll have to be docked for the days of work you missed. This will take care of it, plus overtime for evenings and the weekend. As to the clothes, whatever do you suppose Mr. Corey would do with them? I don't think a secondhand frock would make a very likely birthday gift for one of his friends, do you? Just consider them part of your payment. And you must tell me—were they a success?"

"Oh, yes," Lynne breathed. "That is, I loved wearing them."

"Did you have an opportunity to wear the dinner dress?"

"Yes, there were guests down on Saturday evening for dinner. Mr. Corey wanted me to make an even number at table."

"Oh, yes, Saturday evening. I believe Mrs. Grant

44

was one of the party. Did you two take to one another?"

There was a flicker behind Lynne's eyes as she remembered Justine Grant's hostility. She tried to think of a tactful answer.

Suddenly Madelaine's laugh rippled. "Oh, dear, I seem to sense that you didn't."

Lynne realized that Madelaine was pleased about it, and then she remembered the look of amusement in her eyes as she was selecting the clothes. Astonished, she said, "Why, you meant it to happen that way, didn't you? That's why you decided on the blue dress, because you thought it looked pretty enough that she'd be annoyed!"

"What an imagination you have! Why on earth would Justine Grant mind if there was another attractive woman around to share a little of the attention? And what difference would it make to me if she did?"

But there was still laughter in Madelaine's voice, and Lynne knew she had been right. Attractive clothing had been chosen instead of merely serviceable things in order, in some way, to score off Justine—perhaps only to annoy her; perhaps in hopes of getting her to reveal herself as a jealous cat. But why? Was Madelaine in love with her employer? Did she want to show up Justine's true colors in hopes of coming between the two?

Lynne felt disturbed. Somehow she had been made a pawn in a game to which she didn't know the rules.

Their food arrived and as the waiter served them, Madelaine asked, "Tell me about the little boy. I understand you got along well with him."

"Oh, yes," Lynne cried. "He's a darling. I miss him already. It's funny—I only knew him a week but it seems so much longer because we spent so much time together. I was the only one he could communicate with; it seemed to accelerate our friendship. Poor little lamb. I feel so sorry for him. I hope his mother recovers."

"How is it you happen to speak Italian so well?"

Lynne didn't like talking about it, but her relationship with Madelaine Cheney seemed accelerated too, so she said, "I was studying to be an opera singer. I speak French and German, too."

"And you've given it up?"

Lynne gave a mirthless little laugh. "You're listening to this raspy voice and asking if I've given it up? Yes, I had an accident to my laryngeal nerve and I can no longer sing."

If there was sympathy in the other woman's eyes, she took care not to show it. Instead she said, "Your voice isn't raspy. It's just a little husky. Actually it's quite attractive—rather sensuous."

Now Lynne laughed in earnest. "Somehow I've never thought of myself in those terms."

"How did you wind up at the Corey Company?"

Lynne told her about Uncle Simon, about his determination that she take a business course, and about her determination to pay off her debt to him and eventually to go back to school so she could qualify to teach languages. "That's why the notion of working overtime was so attractive to me," she explained. "It brings me one step closer to being free of that debt. At least," she added with a self-conscious moue, "it was attractive until I became suspicious of your high-handed employer."

"But it all worked out for the best after all, didn't it?" Madelaine's eyes searched Lynne's.

"I wouldn't have missed meeting Tonio for anything," Lynne said. If it was not a full answer to the question, it was the only answer she could give.

* * *

Jason Corey rubbed a weary hand over his face. Four days earlier he had attended the funeral of his sister-in-law, Francesca D'Allasio Corey. She had suffered a relapse two weeks after Tonio had been taken to her and his grandparents in Madrid.

The intervening days had been spent in arguments, legal tangles, and frustrations.

"The situation is impossible, Darren. You can understand that," Jason said to his legal advisor. "I can't leave the boy with his grandparents indefinitely, He's my brother's son—he's English. And I'm his closest relative."

"I understand your feeling well enough," Darren said, "but it's a sticky proposition. The fact is that the boy is in Italy with grandparents who don't want to give him up. You'll have to convince an Italian judge, not me. It's a pity he ever went back to Italy at all."

"That's water under the bridge, Darren. I couldn't keep the boy from his mother after she came out of the coma and wanted to see him. At that time there seemed a good hope for her recovery. And I couldn't keep him away from her funeral in Florence—even if I had had any idea there was going to be a custody battle."

"I'll tell you one thing, Jason. As a bachelor, you're not going to stand a chance of convincing an Italian judge that you ought to have the boy."

"And yet you assured me that Justine won't be free for at least a year."

"That's right."

"I can't let it drag on for a year. One point in our favor is that Tonio never actually lived with his grandparents, since they were in Florence, while Morgan, Francesca, and Tonio lived in Turin. But if we

47

leave him with them for a year, it'll be that much harder to uproot him—and to convince the courts that it's a good idea to uproot him. Besides, the younger he is, the quicker he'll learn English and English ways. It'll be harder for him the longer we wait."

"Well, you could always marry someone else, Jase," Darren said half-jokingly. Then he sobered. "You know that isn't a bad idea. A marriage now—strictly a business proposition, of course. And then, when all the legal ties are snugly knotted with Tonio and you're safely back in England, a quiet divorce."

"You can't be serious! What woman would agree to such a proposal?" he scoffed. "It would have to be the right kind of a woman or we wouldn't be able to convince a court that I was fit to raise the boy. And I can't see that sort of woman agreeing to such a farce. Besides, what would Justine say?"

"Justine can't marry you for a year anyway. Surely she cares enough about what's important to you to go along with what would only be a charade." There was an odd, indefinable tone in his voice. "A reasonable woman with your best interests at heart couldn't object—when she considers what's at stake."

"You're really serious about this, aren't you?" Jason asked incredulously.

"Can you think of another solution?"

Jason spun his chair around to face the window and stared sightlessly over the city for some minutes. "Even if I were to agree," he said at last, "and I emphasize if, where would we find a woman without other attachments, an honest woman who wouldn't take advantage of the situation, someone with the right qualities to impress a judge?"

There was a sudden gleam in Darren's eye. "It

wouldn't hurt if she spoke Italian and was already acquainted with the boy either, would it?"

Jason stared at him in astonishment. "You mean the little clerk-typist—"

"I mean the little clerk-typist whose manners are delightful, who speaks fluent Italian, whom the boy is fond of, and—who is quite a dish."

"It wouldn't work," Jason said thoughtfully. "A clerk-typist ought to take direction from the head of her company without argument, but this one's—independent. She seemed to take an aversion to me."

"Well, maybe you can mend your fences, old boy."

"Besides, for all I know she has a jealous boyfriend."

"Call Maddy in," Darren suggested. "She has a good instinct about people."

Jason buzzed for Miss Cheney.

"Maddy, we need your opinion on a personal matter," Darren said as she entered the room. "A woman's viewpoint."

"What we need is for you to convince this legal eagle that he's out of his mind," Jason put in.

Darren ignored him. "Here's the situation." He outlined the idea for her and sat back, waiting expectantly.

"And what is it, exactly, that you want from me?" asked Miss Cheney.

"We want you to tell us whether you think a woman would agree to such a proposal, whether Lynne Delevan would be the right one. Or we want you to suggest a more suitable candidate, if you have one."

She looked very thoughtful, considering. "I think in many ways Lynne would be an ideal candidate, but I'm not sure she'd agree. It would take gentle handling."

"Why do you say that?"

"I think it would go against the grain with her to do anything that she considered dishonest."

Darren looked deflated.

"However," she went on, "if she could be convinced it's in a good cause— She's genuinely devoted to the boy, I know that. If she really thought it was in his best interest—"

"And how do you know of this devotion to Tonio?" Jason asked.

"We had lunch together just after she came back from Longridge. She wanted to ask me what she should do with the clothes."

Jason blinked. "The clothes?"

"Yes, she didn't think she should keep them. She said the cheque was too generous. She felt guilty about the money that had been spent on the clothes."

"Well, there's an indication of her honesty," Darren said in triumph.

"But there is one other thing." She paused. "I'm afraid she thinks Mr. Corey is rather high-handed. I'm not sure but what she wouldn't consider this further evidence of it—the idea of hiring a wife for half a year or so. It does have a rather lordly ring to it. You know—as if you thought you could just snap your fingers and expect a girl to jump into matrimony."

Jason flushed with annoyance. "It wouldn't precisely be matrimony. It would just be a job. I thought that point was clear. However, I agree, she's not suitable."

"But she is," Darren insisted. "In fact she's your only living link with Tonio. It was obvious how crazy he was about her that weekend I saw them together. Think how much more compelling it would be if you had a wife Tonio was already fond of."

"But from what Maddy says, she'd never agree. We're just wasting our time discussing it."

"I didn't say she wouldn't," Madelaine commented. "I just said it would take careful handling. I know she does need money."

"What's a girl like that doing in a typing pool anyway?" Darren demanded.

Madelaine decided against revealing the whole story. "Her parents died and she fell on hard times. An old curmudgeon of an uncle with a bee in his bonnet about the business world offered to support her through a secretarial course; it was that or starve. But a business office is not what she's fitted for, by any stretch of the imagination. So now she's working and slowly paying off her debt to her uncle, after which she hopes to support herself through some courses which would qualify her to teach languages in a school. It's going to be a long haul."

"And if taking on this job would mean money to pay off her uncle and take her courses—" Darren said excitedly.

"If she could be convinced, I think she's the perfect choice," Madelaine said. "Would you like me to sound her out? More or less prepare her for your proposition?"

"Splendid idea, Maddy," Darren said. "Sensitive girl like that—Jason's bound to put a foot wrong."

"Wait a minute, you two," Jason interrupted. "Before you rush out and buy a ring, I haven't agreed yet. You both seem very eager to foist this girl off on me."

Darren turned an innocent gaze on him. "Foist her off! Well, I like that! I'm merely trying to choose the best possible candidate to help you get custody of Tonio. If you have someone in mind that you prefer, go ahead."

"No," Jason said slowly. "I have no one else in

mind. This is just happening very fast. I'm wondering how Justine is going to react."

"Jase, if you decide to hire a temporary and purely legal wife to help you gain custody of Tonio, well, it is your decision, isn't it? Not Justine's. And if you're going to do it, what possible objection could Justine have to this girl over any other?"

There was a long, silent moment. Then Jason said, "Very well. It's settled then. Will you speak to her, Maddy?"

"Certainly, sir. I'll do my best." As she rose to leave, her eyes met Darren Lloyd's in a moment of wordless communication.

"That is absolutely preposterous!" Two spots of color burned on Lynne's pale cheeks as she sat facing Madelaine Cheney in the same restaurant where they had had lunch before. Tonight Madelaine had requested a booth in a quiet corner.

"It's not preposterous in the least," Madelaine said firmly. "It's eminently sensible. Think of it—money to repay your uncle, money to study for your teaching degree, all at one stroke. No more typing pool. And a trip to Italy thrown in."

"But marriage!" Lynne protested, her mind reeling from the suddenness of it.

"I've explained to you it would be marriage only in a legal sense. You're being employed to act a role temporarily, nothing more. Good heavens, if you played the role of Mimi in *La Bohème* you wouldn't really expect to have to get consumption, would you? This is just acting. Don't worry about the marriage part. It's only a formality."

"But it seems so—dishonest."

"Now, look here, my girl. Morgan was young and high-spirited. He was living in Italy because he was a test driver for an Italian motor car company. He never expected to make it a lifetime career. He had every intention of quitting and coming back to take his place in the family firm and bringing his son up as an Englishman. Why, he had put him down for his own school practically as soon as Tonio was born. It's only through a tragic act of fate that his plans were interrupted. Mr. Corey's trying to do what his brother would have wanted. Is that so terrible?"

"No, I suppose not," Lynne said slowly, "but still, it is trickery, and I suppose his grandparents must love him very much."

"Perhaps," Madelaine said briskly, "and perhaps a great part of their motive for wanting to keep him is that they'd prefer to have an Italian grandson to an English one. Don't forget, they didn't live in the same town—it's not as if he would be torn from the arms of people who had raised him. And there's Tonio's welfare to think of. They're his grandparents, after all, a whole generation removed from his parents. And he's a lively, normal, noisy little boy, isn't he? Quite a handful for grandparents to manage. Also think of this. If something happens to them, or when Mr. Corey eventually marries in earnest, he'll surely get guardianship and Tonio will be uprooted again. Isn't it better for him to have this happen only once, while he's still young enough to make the adjustment easily?"

"It seems like playing God," Lynne said unhappily. "How can I be sure Mr. Corey is the right one to be Tonio's guardian?"

"Tonio's father was his brother," Madelaine said patiently. "He's the natural choice. Besides, you aren't the one making the judgment. If you don't agree to do the job, someone else will."

"Then why me?" Lynne asked.

"Because Tonio loves you already."

Lynne was silent a long time. Finally she said, "I promise to consider it seriously."

"Consider it quickly," Madelaine advised. "Remember, I told you before, when you have to make up your mind quickly, you'll find you can do it."

On the street in front of the restaurant Lynne took Madelaine's arm and turned to face her. "Why not you, Madelaine? You're wholly devoted to Mr. Corey. You could do it without all this soul-searching."

Madelaine's gaze went quite opaque for a moment. Then she gave a wry smile. "Because, my dear child, I don't want to make either of us ridiculous. He's thirty-one; I'm forty-three. So don't get the wrong idea. I'm devoted to him, but it's his welfare I'm interested in. I just want what's best for him—not the man himself."

Lynne went home to her small flat and crawled into bed to stare into the darkness. She knew sleep would be impossible. Her mind was in turmoil such as she had not known since the day she had finally learned that she would never sing again. But for that she had had weeks of fear to prepare her for the final verdict. This—this was a bolt from the blue and it took her breath away.

"One door closes and another opens," Madame Bertelli had said. Was this chance to pay off her debt to her uncle and make a start on a new career the first crack of light through a new door that was opening?

CHAPTER FIVE

Following Miss Cheney's advice, Jason Corey had his talk with Lynne at dinner, rather than summoning her to his office. "There's something rather daunting about you when you're behind your desk. You seem to be issuing orders rather than making requests," she had said.

His brow lifted. "It's a wonder I've been able to keep such loyal employees."

"Oh, I'm not easily daunted," she had replied. "But this is a different and much more delicate matter than office routine."

And so they were sitting in an excellent, quiet restaurant with two icy cold martinis in front of them.

Lynne twisted the stem of her glass nervously. She had rather obstinately refused to wear any of the new clothes that Jason Corey's money had paid for. She had wanted to be completely her own woman while they talked. She was wearing a simple white blouse and black skirt but she had knotted a soft coral scarf around her neck which softened the effect.

"Knowing Miss Cheney's efficiency, I'm sure she explained the situation thoroughly."

She nodded, not giving him any help.

"Darren Lloyd has studied the matter and he's convinced this is the only way. Francesca's parents refuse to give the boy up. I can't say that I blame them. He's all they have left of Francesca. And there may be—other factors. However, though I'm sorry for the loss of their daughter, it's Tonio who matters most, because his life is ahead of him.

"I know this is what Morgan would have wanted. The last time we saw each other, we discussed his fascination with the test-driving job, but he told me that he had had about enough and was almost ready to pack it in and come home. 'When Tonio starts school, it should be an English one,' is what he said.

"Francesca was driving when the accident happened," he said irrelevantly, his voice suddenly going hoarse.

Lynne maintained a sympathetic silence, giving him a chance to recover.

"I wish it could be done straightforwardly," he said, "but Darren has convinced me that without a wife I don't stand a chance of getting the boy. Strange, isn't it? If Francesca had been killed outright, along with my brother, none of this would have been necessary. When I brought the boy home, he'd simply have stayed. No English court would have questioned it. But it would have been too cruel not to let him see his mother after she regained consciousness. And it seemed only right that he should go back with his grandparents for the funeral.

"But now, distasteful as the idea of subterfuge is, the imperative thing is to get Tonio back in England, at Longridge where he belongs. The D'Allasios are not the right ones to bring the boy up, believe me, Lynne."

What a good executive he is, she was thinking, cutting right to the matter of Tonio's needs, and not trying to tempt me with talking about how I'll benefit from the arrangement. Madeleine has doubtless told him I feel guilty and uncomfortable about going through a psuedo-marriage in order to trick an Italian court, so he's not even mentioning that if I go along with this, it will mean a new start for me, a new life. He knows I'm fond of the boy and want what's best for him.

"After we have him home," Jason said confidently (she noted it was not if, but when) "you are the perfect choice to help him bridge the gap. You can teach him English, prepare him for school. Once he's in school making friends with the other boys his age, he'll do fine, don't you agree? So if you could stay on for a while—"

She felt a surge of annoyance. There he was, manipulating her. If you could stay on for a while. She hadn't even agreed to the first part of the plan.

The waiter brought their Dover sole, perfectly grilled, with a delicate shrimp sauce. Jason applied himself to the food, not mentioning Tonio again. Through the fish and well into the roast beef, he spoke only of impersonal matters, the resignation of an MP, the Queen's visit to Scotland, the ugliness of a new high-rise office building.

But all the time the question lay between them, stretching Lynne's emotions tighter and tighter until suddenly, almost without premeditation, she gasped, "All right, I'll do it."

He laid down his knife and fork and sat back looking at her. He raised his wine glass. "To a successful venture, Lynne, for both of us."

She picked up her glass but she couldn't taste the wine. It was surely the strangest engagement toast any girl had ever had.

To a successful venture.

They had agreed that the quietest possible ceremony was the proper way to do it, with only Madelaine Cheney and Darren Lloyd as witnesses. "A quiet wedding won't be thought odd with my brother so recently dead."

It was to take place as soon as it could be arranged, so they met only once more beforehand. "I'll give you a cheque for your trousseau," he said.

"You've already bought my trouseau, J-Jason"— she stumbled over using his Christian name—"before I came down to Longridge."

He started to object, but seeing the stubborn set of her mouth, he subsided. "Well, you can shop in Paris, then. That might be more fun for you anyway."

"Paris?" she asked, surprised.

"Yes, we're going to drive to Florence—on our honeymoon tour. I think it would look rather suspicious if we suddenly married and descended immediately on the D'Allasios, don't you? I'm cabling them about our marriage, telling them we're touring the continent and hope to visit them and Tonio en route."

"You think of everything, don't you?" she said slowly.

"Not quite. I nearly forgot to give you this." He took a small blue velvet box from his pocket and opened it.

It held a perfect, emerald-cut diamond ring, the stone set simply in platinum with no adornment. "I thought a plain stone would be easier for you to have reset later," he explained, "if you should like to have it made into a dinner ring perhaps."

Her eyes misted. It was hardly the moment a girl dreamed of, receiving her engagement ring—a breathtakingly beautiful ring, too, just what she would have chosen—and all the while being told it had been selected because it would be easy to reset when the marriage was over.

As if she'd keep it afterward! Let him get it reset himself—for Justine.

Why had she let herself get involved in this deception? It was all wrong. If, sometime in the distant future, she should fall in love with someone who loved her, and marry, some of the beauty of it would be spoilt because of this. She had already had an engagement toast ("To a successful venture") and now she had been given a ring. No other ring would be as beautiful as this, and yet this one meant nothing.

The tears in her eyes refracted the lights of the facets on the diamond, splintering them into tiny points of green, blue, and gold, each sharp enough to pierce her heart.

When he saw that she was not going to take it out of the box, he did so himself and slid it on her finger. If only it had been too large or too small, she thought in wild, unreasonable protest. Why did he always have to be so inhumanly efficient?

Before she went to pieces completely, she fled.

The day before the ceremony Madelaine Cheney came to her flat. "I'm bringing you a wedding gift from Mr. Corey," she had said on the phone. What in the world now? Lynne had thought. She was no bride in the true sense of the word, and surely she'd made it clear she wasn't out to get more than their agreement had called for, which was merely the money to pay back Uncle Simon, and afterward to get started in a teaching career, with living expenses in between. So why was he sending her a bridal gift?

When she opened the door to Madelaine, she saw that Johnson, Jason's chauffeur, was standing behind her on the landing.

"Put them inside, Johnson," Madelaine directed,

"and then you can go. I'll be staying on for a bit."

Johnson carried in several huge parcels and a smaller one. After setting them down and wishing her a good day, he left.

Lynne looked at them in perplexity and finally, at Madelaine's urging, started stripping the paper from one of them. It proved to be a magnificent piece of blue leather luggage, the other parcels containing matching pieces.

"Oh, dear, they must have cost the earth! They are lovely. I suppose you chose them."

"As a matter of fact, I didn't," Madelaine said. "I'm only delivering them. I was coming to see you anyway because I have a little gift for you myself." She put a beautifully wrapped, flat white box in Lynne's hands.

"Oh, Madelaine," Lynne cried. "I wish everyone wouldn't keep treating me like a bride, instead of like a partner in a business arrangement. It makes me feel so—so dishonest."

"There you go being tiresome again," Madelaine said briskly. "Where does it say business can't be enjoyable?"

Lynne untied the white satin bow but, before she could lift the lid of the box, Madelaine laid her hand on it. "Before you open it and start protesting, let me say at once that it's intended for the benefit of the hotel waiters."

"What?" Lynne said, puzzled. She opened the box to reveal the loveliest negligee she had ever seen, chiffon in a pattern of misty swirls of blue, lavender, and turquoise. She gasped in delight, but then her eyes flew to Madelaine's in dismay.

Madelaine turned back a fold of the chiffon. "You see? It's lined. Fully opaque. High necked. So it's quite proper. I didn't know if you had thought about it, but in France and Italy the hotels are seldom prepared for people coming down to breakfast. They expect to bring a tray to your room. And I thought that brown robe we chose for you to take to Longridge was just too utilitarian for a bride to wear. You don't want waiters all over the continent thinking Mr. Corey has a drab and dreary bride, do you? But this is not at all revealing, so it's very proper," she said emphatically.

Lynne laughed. "I know you're making fun of me, and you're right. I guess I have been acting like a prig. You're a dear to give me such a beautiful gift. I don't know how to thank you."

"Don't try. Perhaps someday you'll be able to do something that will—gratify me highly," Madelaine said.

Lynne was puzzled, wondering what she could mean, but then she forgot all about it as she discovered that with the negligee was a nightgown of matching chiffon. She held up the soft transparent wisp of color, saying mischievously, "I suppose this is perfectly proper, too?"

"Well, they came as a set." Madelaine had a twinkle in her eye. "And you don't need to let anyone see you in it—unless you want to."

The next day dawned fine and clear.

It had been a point of pride with Lynne to buy her own dress for the wedding ceremony and the flight to Paris. She had felt horribly extravagant, but traveling with Jason would be first class all the way, she knew, and she didn't want him to be ashamed of her. She had used her last salary cheque and her small emergency fund to buy her outfit.

She wore a raw silk suit dress with a soft cowl neckline in an apricot shade which lent a becoming bloom to her complexion and brought out the golden glints in her ash-blond hair.

She saw in Jason's eyes that he approved of her appearance. He gave her white orchids, the first she had ever had, and if her hand was trembling as he slipped the plain platinum band on her third finger, he took no notice.

After the simple ceremony, the wedding party adjourned for a festive luncheon. Darren kept up a flow of light conversation and Lynne smiled and nodded at appropriate times, trying not to let her inner turmoil show.

Darren drove them to Heathrow. Johnson would drive one of Jason's cars to the ferry at Calais and deliver it to Paris in a few days, but Jason had thought the flight over would be less fatiguing for Lynne. She thought wryly that it might be all too easy to become accustomed to such luxuries if she didn't keep firmly in mind that this was only a brief interlude in her life.

There were clouds beneath them as they crossed the channel. It added to Lynne's sense of unreality to be suspended between a bright blue sky above and a blanket of white clouds below.

When they began their descent and plunged into the cloud cover, Lynne found it so alarming that she closed her eyes, but soon Jason touched her arm and said, "Any minute now you'll have your first glimpse of Paris."

Sure enough, the clouds began to thin; she could see occasional dark patches below, and then only shreds of white, and suddenly there was the city, off on the horizon. She could see the Eiffel Tower, like a tiny toy, and she caught her breath. She did not realize it at first, but she had reached out instinctively and caught Jason's hand.

He held it firmly in his until the plane touched down.

With his customary efficiency, Jason got them through customs, and had their luggage collected and loaded into a taxi.

The outskirts of the city were somewhat disappointing; they could have been the suburbs of any large city. But once they were in the old part of town, Lynne gazed with delight on the wide avenues, the huge trees, the mellow creamy stones of the buildings.

Their hotel was on the Rue de Rivoli. As Jason helped her out of the taxi he said, "The park across the street is the Tuileries Gardens, and just over there is the Louvre."

Jason checked them in and when the desk clerk said, "I hope you have a pleasant stay, Madame," she tried not to look startled. It was the first time she'd been called Madame. Mrs. Corey. Mrs. Jason Corey. What an improbable sound it had.

One uniformed porter took them up in the lift; another would follow with the luggage. Their suite had two bedrooms. The first was large, light, and airy with a huge carved wardrobe and a delightful antique desk in front of one window.

"Would you like this room?" Jason asked.

"It's lovely," she said, but then she glanced into the second bedroom and saw that, while it was smaller and had only one window, the bed was an antique-style four poster with gold brocade curtains. "Oh, could I have this one please? When I was a child I used to dream of sleeping in a bed like that—like a princess. I'll feel like Catherine de Medici!"

He laughed aloud. She looked at him quickly, but he did not seem to be making fun of her. "What is it?" she asked. "You look so pleased."

"Do you realize," he said, "that that is the first

thing you've ever asked of me? Usually it's 'No, Jason, I don't need that,' or 'Whatever you'd like, Jason.' This is really a milestone—the first time you've shown a preference."

She was silent, thinking about what he had said, and he added, "I like being able to do something to please you."

She was filled with dismay. He had done many thoughtful things; had she seemed so ungrateful, then? She started to speak but then the man arrived with the luggage and the moment was lost.

"I'll give you twenty minutes to unpack and freshen up and then we'll go out for dinner. Don't change. You look perfect just as you are."

As the taxi drew up to the restaurant he had chosen, he said, "I thought we'd save the *grand luxe* restaurants for later. This little one happens to be a special favorite of mine."

And no wonder, she thought. It was small and cozy, the linen snowy, the service perfect. "The pâté maison is excellent here," he said. She found he was right. Everything was delicious. He ordered champagne and this time the toast he proposed was "To your happiness, Lynne."

"And to yours, Jason," she said, feeling very touched.

After the leisurely meal he asked, "Are you too tired to walk a bit?"

"No, I'd like that."

She was surprised then when he hailed a taxi, but the direction he gave to the driver was "Place de la Concorde."

"I thought it would be pleasant to walk around the square," he explained to Lynne.

"I must have seen a thousand pictures of Cleopatra's Needle," she said as they stood at its base looking up at it, "but it's impossible to realize how impressive it is, how huge this whole plaza is, until you see it."

"I wanted you to see it first at night," he said. "The Parisians have lit this city so beautifully. Notre Dame at night is another must."

They circled the *place*, then walked slowly back to the hotel under the arcade of the Rue de Rivoli.

When they reached their suite, Lynne had anticipated an awkward moment, but in a matter-of-fact way Jason asked what time she'd like breakfast sent up. "Good night, then, Catherine de Medici; sweet dreams in your regal bed."

She laughed and went into her room, not feeling embarrassed after all.

Still, she thought, after she had bathed and brushed her hair and put on the gown that had been Madelaine's gift to her, still it was a very strange wedding night. Paris, illuminated with its soft white lights, was magnificent for anyone. What must it be like to share it with someone you loved—on a real honeymoon?

CHAPTER SIX

Lynne awoke, rested and refreshed, ten minutes before the breakfast tray was due. She could not remember having any dreams at all, regal or otherwise.

She splashed cold water on her face, brushed her touseled hair into shape, and took the new negligee off its hanger. Suddenly she was glad to have something pretty to wear. Paris was too beautiful to greet in the morning looking drab. She giggled to herself at the irrationality of the thought.

She heard the door buzzer from the hallway, and then Jason knocked on her door. She opened it to find the waiter putting the tray on the little antique desk. Jason drew up two chairs.

"Oh, Jason, I didn't realize—you can see the Eiffel Tower from this window. Imagine, the Eiffel Tower! How can it look so absurd and so pretty at the same time?"

"Distance lends enchantment," he said in an amused tone. "Well, what shall it be today, sightseeing or shopping?"

"Oh, sightseeing, please."

"Now, how did I know you were going to say that?" he teased.

"Well . . . I've shopped before, but I've never gone sightseeing in Paris."

"Ah, but you've never shopped in Paris either. Caught you that time."

"Touché. However, could we possibly take one of

those little boats on the Seine? It's so sunny today, and who knows, it might rain tomorrow."

"The *vedettes?* Yes, of course. They have larger boats that serve dinner, if you'd like to do that one night. I've never tried it, so I can't vouch for the food, but the boats look very romantic gliding along all lit up. Would you like to go up the Eiffel Tower, by the way?"

"Oh, Jason, I'd rather not. I'm sure you're right about distance lending enchantment. I should think all that bare steel would be ugly close up. Besides, I'm a terrible coward about heights."

She tried one of the croissants. "Mmm, delicious."

"Let's see what we have in the way of jams," he said, peering at the little individual glass pots and reading from the labels. *"Fraise, framboise, cerise."*

"Framboise, please."

"Ah, the perfect traveling companion, who leaves the *fraise* for me," he said, spreading strawberry jam on his croissant.

It was strange, she thought, but he was a good traveling companion, too. He was knowledgable, eager to please her, and yet at the same time tactfully impersonal. She felt grateful to him for making this so much easier than she had feared. He was not being the arrogant man of business that she had first disliked. Nor was he allowing her to feel any embarrassment over the intimacy of their situation. It was as if they were merely a pair of friends off on holiday.

The next few days were a kaleidoscope in Lynne's mind. They wandered through the picturesque streets of Montmartre and visited the Sacre Coeur. They went to the dome of the Invalides in which Napoleon's great porphyry sarcophagus lay enshrined. They visited the book stalls across from Notre Dame and spent an afternoon in the cathedral. Lynne felt as if she were drowning in the glorious light streaming through the magnificent stained-glass windows.

On the way back to the hotel she said, "I've been walking your legs off and you've seen all these things before. You must be tired and bored to death."

"A person would have to be quite blasé to be bored by Paris," he told her. "Besides, when you see it through the eyes of another person, it's fresh and new all over again."

As they stopped for the room key, the desk clerk handed Jason a message. He glanced at it; his face changed and he folded it quickly.

"Bad news?" she asked.

"No, just business. I'm going to have to call London. Maybe you'd like to go to that little *terrasse* around the corner and have coffee or a *citron pressé*. I'll join you when I can."

"Of course," she said instantly.

Sipping the cool, sweet *citron,* she thought that whatever the call was, he didn't want to chance having her overhear from her bedroom. Could it have been Justine calling? It would hardly be remarkable if she wanted to keep tabs on him. It must be infuriating for her to have her fiancé off on a honeymoon with another woman—no matter how platonic the honeymoon was. Well, she needn't worry about Lynne poaching on her territory. This was a business arrangement, but as Madelaine had said, there was no reason business couldn't have its pleasant side. The unpleasant part would come later, when they met with the D'Allasios and had to resort to subterfuge to convince them that they were a happily married couple.

Resolutely she pushed that thought from her mind.

Jason joined her after half an hour, a worried frown on his face. "Lynne, I'm terribly sorry about this—"

Her heart lurched. What dreadful thing had happened?

"Some urgent business has come up and I have to fly back to London for a day or so. I hate to leave you here alone."

She laughed shakily. "Is that all? Goodness, your face looked like doom."

"Do you think you can manage by yourself?"

"Manage?" She was indignant. "I've been taking care of myself for a long time now. Besides, what more could I ask? I have a place to stay, I speak the language, and I could never run out of things to do in Paris."

His relief at the way she was taking it was almost comical. What had he expected her to do? Throw a tantrum? Even if she had been his wife in fact as well as by law, she'd never have done that. What sort of women was he used to?

They went out for an especially elegant dinner that night. She wore her blue dress. As they said good night at her door he added, "I'm catching an early flight, so I won't take time for breakfast here." He reached in his pocket and drew out some franc notes. "Here's some pocket money. You probably won't want to carry a lot so I've left more at the desk. Just ask for it as you need it."

"Thank you," she said. "Have a good trip."

There seemed to be real regret in his eyes as he said, "I'm so sorry I have to go."

"Well, business is business," she said and went into her room. And that's what I am, too, she thought. A business arrangement. Was it really his work that called him home, or was it Justine, calling him to heel? Was he hurrying off in the morning to placate her? Or perhaps he just felt the need to see her again, to have some real pleasure after the tiring business of showing his pseudo-wife the tourist spots of Paris.

Odd how disquieting that thought was. After all, Lynne had no emotional claims on him, nor would she want to have. He was just a business arrangement to her, too, she thought defiantly.

When she woke the next morning, she immediately thought of visiting the Louvre. They had been saving that to do in case it rained because it was so close they could just nip over and spend the day indoors.

The sun was bright today, however. Strange that she should have thought of the Louvre first thing, just as if it had been a rainy day.

It didn't take Lynne long to realize that one could spend a week in this building and never see half of what was in it.

She supposed a visit here wouldn't be complete without viewing the Mona Lisa. When at last she found the right gallery, she was disappointed in the painting. It was so heavily protected, doubtless because of its having been stolen some years ago, that it was hard to see it properly. Anyway, she had always thought the girl had an insipid look, no matter how much she admired da Vinci's brushwork.

She found other, less famous paintings which she enjoyed more and spent the hours until one o'clock wandering through one gallery after another, until she felt so satiated that she decided she had had enough art for one day.

After a small lunch at a sidewalk café near the hotel, she decided it would be a good time to visit the Tuileries Gardens. It had been an unusually warm autumn. The air felt almost summery with only a hint of crispness in the early mornings and late afternoons.

Lynne strolled into the park and admired the lovely trees. Though the flower beds were too manicured and precise to suit her taste, she had to admit they were effective. She walked on until she came to a large round cement pond where some small children were sailing toy boats, pushing them off from the edge with sticks and rushing around to the other side to catch them as they landed.

Smiling, she sat down in a conveniently placed chair to watch. One dark-haired youngster reminded her of Tonio.

Suddenly she felt a surge of longing to see him. It was strange how in the few short days they had been together he had become so dear to her. She had missed him terribly when Jason took him to Spain.

She wished it were all over, the confrontation with the D'Allasios, the legal technicalities, and that they were back at Longridge. She would enjoy being a sort of glorified governess for him—teaching him English, going for rambles through the woods. She wondered if he could ride a pony. There were no stables at Longridge, but perhaps there were ponies for hire somewhere nearby. What fun it would be to teach him to ride, like a proper English boy.

Then a thought smote her and turned the day gray. If she had missed him that much after only a week, what would it be like to lose him after a matter of months? For lose him she would. There would be no friendly visits to Longridge to keep in touch with Tonio when Justine was mistress there!

She was so deep in her unhappy reverie that at first she didn't realize anyone was speaking to her. Then she looked up at the dumpy woman in a park attendant's uniform, who was demanding to know if she'd paid the fee for using the chair. How idiotic, Lynne thought, opening her purse and handing her the smallest note she had. As the woman handed her a ticket and her change and moved off, Lynne looked down at the coins in her hand. "*Arrêtez-vous!*" she called sharply. "You haven't given me the proper change."

Grumbling, the woman returned and grudgingly put another coin in Lynne's outstretched hand.

If that wasn't the limit, Lynne thought crossly. Charge you for sitting down and then try to cheat you in the bargain.

She watched as the attendant approached a couple sitting nearby. The man kept shaking his head and the dumpy little attendant kept gesticulating. Finally, he raised his voice as if speaking loudly and clearly would help her to understand, and Lynne heard him saying in an American accent, "I'm sorry. I don't speak French. No *parle*. I don't know what you want."

Lynne called out to him. "It seems you have to pay a fee for sitting in the chairs."

"Oh, right. Thank you." He paid and after the old woman had left, he and his wife looked at one another and broke into helpless laughter, as if having to pay for the privilege of sitting in a park chair were the funniest thing they'd ever encountered.

Somehow it quite restored Lynne's good humor.

She had been putting off thinking how she was going to spend the evening, for though it was true that she could well take care of herself, the idea of an evening alone in Paris was less enticing than finding ways to spend the daytime hours had been. Now it occurred to her that she had been an idiot not to think of it earlier.

She hurried back to the hotel and asked the concierge if it were possible to get an opera ticket for that evening. He made a phone call and came back smiling. *"Oui, Madame. C'est possible."*

She spent a wonderful evening, after all. Jason needn't have worried. She was perfectly resourceful and she certainly hadn't missed him.

When she woke the next morning it really was raining, which she took as an omen that she'd better go back to the Louvre. She ate her breakfast looking out at the leaden skies, thinking that the sudden change in the weather was quite depressing.

She had just finished eating when the phone jangled. It was Jason. "I've finished up here and I'm catching the noon plane. I just wanted you to know I'd be back in time for dinner."

Her heart seemed to be pounding at the surprise of hearing his voice. "Thank you for calling," she said, adding idiotically, "It's raining here."

"Oh, too bad. Maybe you can go to the Louvre."

"I plan to. I'll see you tonight then."

She stared out over the city. Didn't it seem to be lightening up just a bit in the east?

She heard his key in the lock and then he fairly burst through the door. "Well, I'm back." He held out his strong square hands and gripped hers.

She smiled. "So I see."

He looked genuinely glad to see her. Surely he couldn't have just come from Justine with such a smile on his lips for Lynne. For a crazy second she had even thought he was about to kiss her hello, but then he dropped her hands and said exuberantly, "What's on the program for tomorrow?"

She wanted to say, "A picnic for two in the Bois de Boulogne," but she suddenly felt guilty about enjoying herself. Wasn't she beginning to enjoy herself too much? Hadn't she for brief stretches of time almost forgotten why she was here? Instead, she said, "I was thinking, Jason, that perhaps it's time to think about starting for Italy. I saw a little boy in the Tuileries Gardens yesterday who reminded me of Tonio, and I wondered if we should really be dawdling here in Paris instead of going to him."

The light went out of Jason's deep gray eyes. "Perhaps you're right."

To fill the uneasy silence that followed she said, "Did you get your business taken care of satisfactorily?"

He looked blank, as if he'd never heard of business.

"The business that called you back to London," she prompted.

"Oh, that. Yes, that's taken care of." But he seemed preoccupied. A moment ago she had been sure it was business and not Justine which had taken him away from Paris. Now she wasn't so sure.

At dinner that night he asked, "How did you manage to entertain yourself while I was gone? At the desk they gave me back the envelope of cash I'd left for you. They said you'd never asked for any of it at all."

"I didn't need it."

"I never imagined a woman left alone in Paris with a supply of funds couldn't find something to do with it."

"Perhaps I'm not your ordinary, everyday-type woman," she said lightly.

"I'm beginning to realize that," he said slowly.

She could not meet his eyes for long and dropped hers to the wine goblet in her hand. To break the tension she said, "I did do one extravagant thing. I went to the opera last night."

He snapped his fingers. "What a fool I am. I should

have remembered that you liked opera and thought of it myself. Now about tomorrow—there's no putting it off any longer. We are going shopping and that's final.''

She said in a mock-martyred tone, "Well, sometimes we just have to bow to the inevitable."

It was a day of mixed delight and exasperation for Lynne. Who wouldn't enjoy trying on such beautiful clothes? But Jason seemed to feel it necessary to buy everything that was becoming to her and such extravagance made her uncomfortable.

He bought her two evening dresses, a smart black frock, a peasant-style dress in a whisper-soft blue challis print—for no better reason than he said it showed off her pretty neck—a deep turquoise daytime dress, a rust wool suit, and a selection of trouser outfits which he said would be comfortable for driving, and useful later in the country. He topped it off with the purchase of a coat and an evening wrap.

"Jason, how will I ever get all these things into my luggage?" she protested at last.

"We could buy you a new suitcase."

"I was only joking."

"But that reminds me, you will need some handbags. And shoes."

"What, no tiara?"

He laughed. "If you're a good girl and try on your shoes without complaining, you may have a tiara."

"Oh, super," she giggled. "But it must be sapphires and diamonds."

He sighed. "There you go being economical again. I was planning on emeralds."

It was their last night in Paris and it seemed to Lynne that the City of Lights was putting on a special show for them. The sky turned pink and gold behind the Eiffel Tower as they watched from their window.

Then the pink shaded into the softest mauve and finally a deep blue. The air had a luminescent look, and the floodlit buildings looked more romantic than ever before.

They went to Maxime's and Lynne wore her new ivory silk evening dress. Heads turned as they walked in. Jason could always make heads turn, she thought. He walked with such a confident air, his dark hair and penetrating eyes always captured people's attention. His manners were superb as he solicitously ordered for her.

Oh, Jason, she thought, you are so experienced—such a man of the world. I hope you're not going to spoil me for ordinary men.

She had to hold fast to the notion that somewhere in the shadowy future, some nameless, faceless man awaited her. She knew that someday she wanted children—wanted to share her life with someone. Someday she would marry in earnest, though at this moment it was impossible to imagine falling in love. It had never seemed so before, but now it occurred to her, though she could not have said why, that being in love was a condition fraught with danger. She hoped that in the distant time when she did find a man of her own, she would not forever be comparing him with Jason—with Jason's aristocratic looks and strength, with the way Jason could make heads turn and people jump to his bidding.

She shivered.

This strangest of honeymoons was almost over, and Lynne couldn't be sure whether she was glad or sorry.

CHAPTER SEVEN

Johnson had delivered Jason's car and it surprised Lynne. She had been expecting something flashy and low-slung, a rich man's toy. Instead, it was a conservative moss green vehicle, although sleek and elegant, to be sure. Not until they had left the suburbs behind and were out on the open highway did Jason open it up. Lynne realized how much power there was beneath the bonnet.

As the miles fell away, she occasionally glanced at Jason's profile as he maneuvered the car with relaxed concentration.

He seemed to have his mind wholly on the road, but he must have been aware of her scrutiny because he said suddenly, "What are you thinking about so seriously?"

"Nothing serious at all," she said in momentary confusion. "I was just thinking that this car is like Clark Kent."

His brows lifted in astonishment. "Like Clark Kent!"

"Yes. You know. It looks rather ordinary like mild-mannered Clark Kent, until all at once it turns into Superman and takes off like a bird."

He laughed. "I suppose I'll never be able to think of it as anything but Clark Kent again. I wonder how Johnson will take it when I say, 'Johnson, please bring Clark to the front door in five minutes.'"

A little after noon he asked, "Getting hungry?"

"Moderately." Then, struck by a sudden idea, she

asked, "Jason, do you suppose we could have a picnic?" Immediately she was sorry she had mentioned it. Picnics were probably not Jason's style. He liked the excellent service and elegant food of good restaurants.

Surprisingly he pulled off the highway onto a side road, saying, "Your wish is my command."

Yes, she thought, during this brief period, with his gentlemanly manners, her wish did seem to be his command. But she sensed that it would never be wise to seriously cross swords with him. Like his car, his appearance was deceptive. Under the polished exterior lay vast power waiting to be unleashed.

They stopped in the first village they came to and, entering a small shop, chose sharp yellow cheese, paté, grapes, and downy peaches. "And some of the brie," he added as an afterthought. Next door was a *boulangerie* where they bought crusty bread, and then Jason looked up and down the street. "We'll have to find a wine merchant. I have the loaf of bread and thou; I certainly insist on a jug of wine to complete the set."

Ever practical, Lynne said, "What about a knife to cut the cheese and some paper napkins and cups?"

He snapped his fingers. "We should have one of those fitted-out picnic hampers."

"And I thought you were always prepared for everything," Lynne teased. "I'm disappointed."

Their purchases loaded, they drove slowly along the narrow road beyond the village, looking for a likely place to stop.

It was such a beautiful Saturday that there were many other picnickers beside the road. Lynne was amused at the elaborate gear some of them had outfitted themselves with. They passed several families sitting in camp chairs around card tables; one man unloaded a folding lounge chair from the boot of his car while his wife held a portable radio.

"Some people know how to put on a picnic!" she said, still teasing. "Tables, chairs, luncheon music. And we have to make do with a packet of paper napkins."

"The honeymoon's not even over and already she's turning into a nag," he grinned.

Suddenly he swerved off onto an even narrower lane. "Goodness, Jason, this doesn't look as if it leads anywhere. Are you sure we won't get lost?"

"Not absolutely," he said cheerfully. "I just thought there might be a quieter spot along here where you won't see any of those well-equipped picnickers and keep making invidious comparisons."

They rounded a turn and came upon an opening in the trees where a small stream tumbled down a grassy bank. Leave it to Jason to have found the perfect spot. If there were any justice, this lane would have ended up at a rubbish heap. Then she forgot that fleeting notion in her delight at the exquisite scene.

There was a car robe in the boot which Jason spread under a tree. The whisper of the leaves and the gentle gurgling of the stream below was sweeter and more soothing than any music coming from a radio would have been.

Everything tasted delicious, from the sharp golden cheese to the mellow, sun-warmed peaches. "I feel replete at last," Jason said, finishing the last of the soft, creamy brie. "In fact, practically stuporous."

"Why don't you rest a bit?" Lynne suggested. "I'd love to explore the stream."

"That sounds good," he agreed. "Don't go too far."

When she returned, he was asleep with his head pillowed on his folded up jacket. Very gently, so as not to disturb him, she sat down on the edge of the car robe to wait.

He had loosened the top of his shirt and she could see the dark brown hair on his well-muscled chest. He looked so much younger as he slept, all the firmness of purpose, the strength of will, erased from his face. She had never seen him when his hair was not perfectly groomed, but now it was touseled and one lock fell across his forehead. She felt an absurd desire to push it back.

Presently he stirred slightly and before he could open his eyes and see that she was watching him, she quickly busied herself with cleaning up the debris from their picnic lunch.

Back on the main road she asked, "Where are we going to stop tonight?"

"I thought it would be pleasant to spend tomorrow on Lake Annecy. There's a *grand luxe* hotel in the town of Annecy, but if we go around to the other side of the lake to Talloires there's an inn with a fabulous dining room, the Auberge du Père Bise. The inn also has a few rooms, fifteen or sixteen, I think, and I've booked us two for tonight and tomorrow night."

They had to leave the main road as they turned toward Annecy. The terrain grew hillier and the road twisted and turned continually. They ran into a sudden rainstorm, a regular downpour, which the windscreen wipers could hardly take care of, but Jason didn't slacken his pace.

Lynne knew the road must be slippery and she was pale with fright as the car swooped and swerved, up, down, and around sharp curves. She was determined not to say anything to betray her fears but sat clinging to the door handle for dear life. After three-quarters of an hour they ran out of the storm and she let out a long sigh of relief. "Good old reliable Clark Kent," she murmured, patting the dashboard gratefully.

The town of Annecy looked charming but Jason said, "I think we'll drive straight on around to Talloires and get settled in. We can explore Annecy tomorrow."

The *auberge* was delightful, situated right on the edge of the water of one of the most beautiful lakes Lynne had ever seen. It was long and narrow, the water almost an ultramarine blue, and all around it rose lush green mountains.

"We're lucky in the weather," Jason told her. "When it's fine like this, there are tables on the veranda so we can eat directly on the water."

As they were seated at one of the choicest tables, Lynne said, "It's all so beautiful, I hardly know where to look—at the water, the mountains, or at the flowers."

"Look at the colorful sails on those boats," Jason said. "That turquoise one next to the yellow."

"They could serve nothing more than a crust of bread in a setting like this and no one would notice the difference," Lynne said happily.

She was quite wrong about that, however. The Auberge du Père Bise deserved its three stars. When the food arrived, she was happy to concentrate on every delicious morsel.

"That *mousse de foies de volaille* was out of this world," she said. "I hope I'm not eating my way out of my new wardrobe."

Jason glanced at her slender waist. "I don't see any signs of it yet. Tomorrow night we could try a different place for dinner, but this is the only three-star restaurant in the area."

"I'd love to come back here and try the *gratin de queues d'écrevisses*," she said.

Suddenly she started to laugh. "Will you listen to

me? I'm acting as if my life depended on a chance to eat a gratin of crayfish, when all the time I know that if I were at home I'd be delighted with a nice tin of kippers."

"But you aren't at home. You're in Talloires," Jason pointed out, smiling. "So drink up your cognac like a good girl, and we'll take a short stroll and make an early night of it so we can get up early and explore."

The next morning they took a boat trip. Each part of the lake seemed lovelier than the last. The tops of the mountains were a kind of misty blue in the morning light, the water dotted with colorful sails.

They drove down to Annecy for lunch and prowled around the picturesque streets of the old part of town near the water's edge. Great white tubs of brilliant red flowers decorated the marina, as small boats bobbed at their moorings in the water beyond.

Dinner that night at the *auberge* was as marvelous as it had been the night before. In vain Lynne tried to feel guilty at enjoying herself so much. The future and its problems would come soon enough, but for the moment it was impossible not to be relaxed and happy in a place like this.

As they drove away the next morning, Lynne turned with regret from her last glimpse of Lake Annecy. She unfolded the map and studied it. They were heading for Milan. "Which way do we go?" she asked.

"We head for Chamonix and then go through the Mont Blanc tunnel."

The scenery became spectacular as they approached Chamonix, but Lynne considered the tunnel with some trepidation. "Imagine being underground for seven miles with all that great mountain on top of you," she said with a shudder.

"It's not directly on top of you or I admit you'd be rather squashed. It's on top of the tunnel, which is quite another matter. Will it help if I hold your hand as we drive through?"

"Goodness, no. Keep both hands on the wheel. Wouldn't it be awful to have an accident in there? It would probably tie up traffic for miles and how would the ambulance get there?"

He laughed. "You're determined to take a dim view of this, aren't you? Never mind. Mild-mannered Clark Kent will see us through."

Lynne felt even more claustrophobic inside the tunnel than she had expected. The sight of the open sky was glorious at the end, even though it was rather an overcast day and the air was hazy. Still, it couldn't have looked more beautiful to her at that moment if it had been the purest of azures. She was silent for miles and Jason did not try to converse with her. They were well down into the Valle d'Aosta before she began to take her customary interest in their surroundings.

After the gemlike perfection of Annecy and Talloires and the creamy elegance of Paris, Milan seemed dark and dreary.

The traffic pattern in the center of town, which seemed to consist of concentric circles of one-way streets, was confusing in the extreme and Jason was soon swearing under his breath. "Isn't this the same archway we've passed three times already?" he growled. "We may have to get a helicopter lift to set us down in the center of town."

Lynne smiled inwardly. It was reassuring to see that Jason could, after all, make a wrong move.

They found their hotel at last and settled into a suite with a small sitting room between two bedrooms.

Jason looked somewhat weary after the exhausting drive and Lynne was happy to comply when he asked, "Do you mind if we just eat in the hotel and turn in early? Since we'll be here only through tomorrow night, it's going to be a long day if we try to see much of the town."

They would have just tomorrow in Milan, and then the next day Florence—and Tonio.

As they started out the next morning, Jason said, "Of course I know you'll want to see the cathedral first. In fact, we could probably spend the whole day there."

Lynne nodded politely but without much enthusiasm.

Her first sight of it was overwhelming. It was an enormous, soaring structure, every inch of which seemed to be covered with carvings.

"This is the third largest cathedral in Europe," he read from the guide book he had purchased at the hotel desk. "There are one hundred and thirty five spires, each topped with the statue of a saint, and there are nearly three thousand more relief-carved statues on the building proper. Lynne, are you paying attention?"

She had been peering off in another direction but now turned guiltily back. "Oh, uh, yes, of course. The third largest saint in Europe."

He burst into laughter and, taking her arm, turned her around. "All right, I won't tease you anymore. La Scala is down this way."

She gasped. "Jason, you beast! You knew all the time I wanted to see it!"

"Well, since I was reminded in Paris that you're an opera lover, I suspected you might."

The facade was not imposing compared to the

cathedral but to anyone who loved opera it was the penultimate; the dream of every singer was to one day sing there.

"Do you suppose I could persuade you to accompany me to the performance tonight?"

"You mean you have tickets?" There were stars in her eyes.

"I called from Paris to be sure of getting them."

"Oh, Jason, you're an angel! Now I'll go and look at the duomo and count all twelve thousand saints if you like."

Though there was a stern warning at the entrance that all visitors must be modestly dressed, inside the atmosphere was much gayer and more casual than in the French cathedrals. People chatted and waved to each other in a relaxed manner.

A white-robed priest carrying the chalice and followed by an acolyte swinging a censer approached the altar of a small side chapel, but even then the visitors waiting for the mass did not cease their conversation.

Now that she knew she was actually going to La Scala, Lynne could take pleasure in the beauty and grandeur of the duomo. They spent the whole morning there, even going up on the roof to admire the white marble statues.

Afterward they went to the Gallery of Victor Emmanuel, a huge glass-roofed building with small shops along the sides of the wide central passageway. They ate a light lunch at a café which had tables set up in the passage under the glass roof.

"I think I've regained my energy," Lynne said when they had finished. "The guide book says the pictures at the Pinacoteca di Brera are a must. Shall we go there this afternoon?"

* * *

She was too excited to taste her dinner that night. Once inside La Scala, her eyes were wide, memorizing every detail. Just to be within these hallowed walls where so much musical history had been written was joy beyond words. From the four statues of the great Italian operatic composers in the foyer, right down to the lighting fixtures, everything was fascinating to her.

It wasn't until they had been seated for some minutes and she had absorbed every detail of design and decor that she looked at the program in her lap. *Lucia di Lammermoor!* "Lucia," she whispered.

At intermission Jason said, "I'm not as knowledgeable as you, but it sounded excellent to me and the audience seemed enthusiastic. Is this really a first-rate production?"

"Yes, oh, yes." She nodded, too moved to say more.

She was very quiet on the way back to the hotel afterward. As they reached the lobby, Jason turned to ask if she'd like to go into the bar lounge for a drink, and saw that there were tears streaming down her cheeks. Changing his mind, he took her directly up to their suite, and seating her on the settee, phoned for two cognacs to be sent up.

"Tell me what's troubling you, Lynne."

His voice was so gentle and concerned that to her embarrassment the tears came faster. She groped in her bag for a handkerchief.

"Is it something I've done? Are you unhappy with our agreement?"

She shook her head.

"Something to do with the opera?"

"Lucia," she said faintly. "Lucia was the last role I sang—will ever sing."

He stood staring at her in bewilderment, and at that moment the door buzzer sounded. He took the cognacs from the waiter and, putting them on the coffee table in front of her, sat down beside her.

"I don't understand, but I'd like to," he said, handing her one of the glasses. "Try to drink a little of this."

She sipped some of the smooth, warming liquid and wiped her eyes. "I'm so sorry; I'm behaving like a fool. I never dreamed it would affect me that way. I wanted to hear it. I truly did. It just—brought it all back so clearly."

"Brought all what back?"

"I trained to be a singer, since I was a child," she said. "The Maestro under whom I worked sometimes produced opera, using his London students for special festivals in the smaller towns or at universities. We had just done a production of *Lucia di Lammermoor* when our bus was in an accident on the way back to London. There was"—she stopped, choked, and went on—"there was damage to my laryngeal nerve. I can never sing again."

He looked appalled. "Oh, my poor child."

"I was very lucky, they told me," she said carefully. "Because eventually I was able to talk—almost normally. It could have been so much worse. I could have been maimed—or even killed. But I'm perfectly all right, except for just that one little defect—my voice."

She put her face in her hands. "I'm so ashamed of making such a scene. I don't cry about it anymore, not since I found out the final verdict from the doctors. I don't know what came over me tonight."

"It was my fault," he said contritely, "making you listen to that very opera."

"Oh, no," she protested. "I wouldn't have missed going to La Scala for anything. And I still love the opera. I always will. I couldn't have avoided hearing

Lucia forever—I wouldn't even have tried to. I never dreamed I'd act like such a—a baby."

"You're not acting like a baby," he said fiercely. "It's only natural—"

"It's not just that I can't sing," she said, looking up at him through a mist. "Millions of people can't sing. I suppose very few people are able to fulfill their dearest ambition. It's just that—having prepared all my life for that one thing, it seems as if I have no purpose in life now, no spot to fill, nowhere I'm needed. I'm just cast loose—drifting."

Suddenly she broke down and wept and his arms were cradling her, holding her close. She leaned against him as the tears fell, grateful for his solid strength, grateful to be letting out the pain that had been bottled up for so long.

"Of course you have a purpose," he was murmuring. "Of course you're needed." His voice went on comforting and soothing her, and then he was pushing back her hair from her face and his mouth was against her cheek as he went on saying, "My poor little dear."

And then his lips were on hers and it was a comforting kiss, comforting to know someone cared about her unhappiness. She felt as if she was drawing strength from his firm, warm mouth. But then it changed and his lips were no longer gently soothing. They were seeking hungrily and his arms tightened around her, crushing her against him.

She never knew quite how but her arms went around him, one hand to the back of his neck, the other moving across his taut-muscled shoulders, pressing him even closer against her breast.

She was so inexperienced that she was unprepared for the rush of warm excitement that flamed through her body. Her mouth was as eager as his with yearning and searching.

And then abruptly he thrust her away and stood up. She felt as if she had fallen a long way, from a high place into a void.

He went to the window, his back toward her. "I— I don't know what to say, Lynne." His voice was hoarse. "I didn't intend to— I don't know how it happened. I know we had an agreement, and I swear I meant to keep it. I'm bitterly ashamed. Please believe that. It won't happen again."

She was reeling from the double shock of her awakened emotions and now from his rejection of her. Bitterly ashamed. Of course he was embarrassed, making love, even for just a moment, to a nobody like her with whom he had a purely business agreement, as he had just reminded her.

"Can you forgive me?" He turned toward her now, painfully. "I never meant to— It was just that you were so—"

"So maudlin and weeping on your shoulder," she said. She never knew afterward how she kept her voice even. "Of course I understand. There's nothing to forgive. It was of no importance."

With her head very high she walked into her own room, shot the bolt, and threw herself across the bed. She squeezed her eyes very tightly together. She could not even allow herself to cry. If he were still in the sitting room he might hear her.

At last she got up and undressed. Automatically she slid into the chiffon nightgown Madelaine Cheney had given her. She looked up and caught sight of herself in the mirror. "What am I?" she whispered. She looked like a wanton. Her hair was wild around her face. Her eyes were inky black. She could see her body through the transparent fabric of the gown, the swelling breasts, the rounded hips, the firm thighs, and every inch of her on fire with longing for the touch of his hands, her whole body aching to strain and press against the hard strength of him, to be devoured, consumed by him.

With a moan she tore off the gown and, scrambling through her suitcase, found a pair of cotton pajamas and put them on.

She got into bed.

She couldn't even hate him; she could only hate herself. It wasn't Jason's fault. He was a healthy, virile man. Their situation of forced intimacy, virtually spending all their time together, had built-in dangers that she had not foreseen. Probably he had not foreseen them either. And when she had broken down and practically forced herself into his arms, no wonder he had responded—for a moment—until he remembered that she was not the girl he was in love with, that she was only an employee.

Right now he was probably filled with disgust at the memory of having held her that way.

If only she could hate him. It would be so much easier, but he had been kind to her, a good companion until that humiliating moment in the other room. No, it was she who was to blame. Her body and her heart had betrayed her. Even now she wanted him, knew that, over the past days, she had fallen irrevocably in love with him.

There was only one small crumb of comfort. Jason would never know.

CHAPTER EIGHT

She had not thought it possible that she would sleep, but at last she did. Mercifully it was a deep and dreamless sleep, but she awoke early. She was glad because it gave her time to sort out her thoughts before she had to face him.

One thing she determined—she was going to have to use every bit of acting ability she possessed. She must pretend that nothing of importance had happened, which meant that she could not allow herself the luxury of drawing into a shell. She must seem as friendly and interested in the sights they were seeing as before, because if he should guess what last night had meant to her, what she had discovered about her feelings for him, her humiliation would be unbearable.

How embarrassing it would be for him, in love with Justine, to discover that the silly girl he had hired to play the part of his bride was taking her role to heart. What an impossible situation.

No, she must give an appearance of normality so that he would never guess how difficult every moment in his company was for her.

She was dressed before she heard the waiter buzz with the breakfast trays. She emerged from her bedroom saying brightly, "I overslept and I'm not packed yet. I'll just have a quick cup of coffee and then go and finish with it."

"There's no hurry," he said mildly. "It's only

about a four-hour drive. There's an *autostrada* we can follow the whole route."

If his eyes were searching her face, she was concentrating too carefully on pouring out her coffee to see it. Only when she sorted through the little tins of jam and automatically pushed his favorite strawberry toward him, did her hand falter, but she quickly recovered.

Choking down one roll, which she could hardly swallow, and gulping the coffee, she escaped to her room to stand and stare bleakly out the window. Her packing had been finished long since.

The impersonal mechanics of checking out and getting the luggage arranged in the boot were welcome distractions. With his customary efficiency, Jason had checked with the concierge on the proper route out of the city to get on the *autostrada*. "So let's hope there's no more driving around in circles the way we did when we came into town," he said.

She took the map out and pretended to study it.

The countryside from the *autostrada* was not very interesting, and a permanent haze dulled the sky from the smoke of the northern Italian industrial works.

Jason drove in the fast lane most of the time and the miles slipped away quickly. When they saw the signs for Parma, he said, "I thought we might have lunch here, but it seems too early. Would you just as soon continue?"

"Yes, I'm not hungry."

It was afternoon when they reached the exits to Bologna. "I think we'll stop here." This time he had no trouble finding the center of town. Though the sun did not seem very bright through the hazy overcast, the day was unseasonably warm and they ate at a *terrazzo* on a picturesque street.

"How soon do you think we'll be able to see Tonio?" she asked.

"That depends on the D'Allasios. I'll call them as soon as we get settled in. Darren thinks it best if we don't make any legal moves immediately. He's hoping it won't be necessary. I'm not as sanguine about it as he is, but he thinks there's a possibility that actually having a five year old in their care these past few weeks may have changed his grandparents' minds about keeping him permanently. After all, it's been years since they had a child in the household full time. He thinks they may realize that their life-style would undergo a drastic change if they plan to raise him."

"Perhaps," Lynne said hopefully.

"I don't think that will happen, but then, too, he thinks if we can establish a good rapport with Tonio, as a couple and as prospective guardians, it will help. So we'll just play it by ear for a while."

After lunch he said, "Do you mind if we take a stroll? I'd like to stretch my legs before we get back in the car."

"Of course I don't mind. Would you like me to drive the rest of the way?"

"No, I'm not tired and it's only a short way farther."

It was not surprising he didn't take her up on her offer, Lynne thought. Jason liked to be in control at all times.

They admired the front of the basilica and Neptune's Fountain and then walked down to the Piazza di Parta Ravegnana and looked at the two strange tilted towers. "I don't suppose you'd care to climb up for the view?" Jason asked.

Lynne stared upward. "It's too soon after lunch for me, but if you'd like to, I'll be happy to wait."

95

"Well, I've always wanted to climb a leaning tower, but I guess I'll save myself in case I ever get to Pisa."

Lynne forced a small smile. It was the closest either of them had come to attempting a casual joke all day. Getting back on the old footing wouldn't be easy, but she would put her best effort into it. She had to. She wondered if he had been relieved that she hadn't made any uncomfortable scene that morning.

The scenery was more attractive now, hillier, with an occasional crumbling red brick palazzo perched high on a shelf of rock above the road.

Even encased in her cocoon of dull misery, Lynne couldn't help feeling a stirring of interest as they drove toward the center of Florence. The city had its share of one-way streets, but this time Jason seemed to know what he was doing, fortified no doubt by more directions from the concierge at the hotel in Milan.

"Now we have to turn back along the Arno and we should be getting to the hotel at any minute."

The Arno! What historic associations this river brought to mind. Then Lynne caught her breath. "There's the Ponte Vecchio! Why, it looks just the way it does in pictures."

"And here's our hotel."

"Jason, you mean we're staying practically right on top of the Ponte Vecchio?"

Their suite turned out to be three rooms on the front facing the river with a superb view of the bridge. Jason had probably requested it that way. Leave it to him to think of everything. Nearly everything. The one thing he hadn't counted on was something he couldn't have been expected to foresee. Lynne resolutely pushed that thought away. From now on she would concentrate very hard on absorbing the sights of Florence—and on Tonio.

By the time she had unpacked, Jason knocked on her bedroom door. "I just talked with Isabella, Signora D'Allasio that is, and she grudgingly invited us to come to see Tonio about five thirty this afternoon. They have a villa between here and Fiesole, so we should allow plenty of time to find it. Will that rush you too much?"

"No, I can change in five minutes."

"They didn't invite us to stay for dinner, so I suppose we must assume we aren't exactly welcome guests," he said wryly.

"I take it that Signora D'Allasio does speak English then."

"Yes, she and Matteo both do, but I don't think they're as fluent as you are in Italian." He frowned. "I wish there were some way we could keep them from knowing that you are so fluent, but with Tonio around that won't be possible."

She was puzzled. "Why don't you want them to know?"

"I'm not sure. It's just a feeling I have that it would be an ace in the hole if they didn't know. People often speak more openly to each other if they think they can't be understood. It might help give us a clue as to their attitude."

"Well, I suppose I could speak only very simple Italian to Tonio when they are around, and in English to them, if you think it would be of any help."

He looked gloomy. "It probably won't work. Knowing you speak any of the language at all will doubtless put them on their guard."

It was a beautiful drive to the D'Allasios' villa, but if Lynne hadn't been so concerned about the first meeting with Tonio's grandparents, she would have enjoyed it more.

The villa was charming, set into a terraced hillside.

It looked old but not all of the same period, as if various owners had added a room or a wing to suit their individual whims.

A neatly uniformed maid showed them in. As they waited, Lynne said in a low tone, "I have butterflies in my stomach. That's absurd, isn't it?"

She had a dreadful feeling that Isabella D'Allasio was going to be some sort of oracle who would take one look at her and know her for the fraud she was.

When her hostess entered the room, Lynne felt stunned surprise. This was hardly the sad-faced, elderly grandmotherly type she had pictured. The woman in front of her was extremely slender, not quite as tall as Lynne, but with a commanding presence. She was dressed all in black, but in a sleekly modish style. She looked to be in her mid-forties. Her carefully made-up face was cool, reserved, giving no hint of what was going on inside her head.

"Signora, it was good of you to let us come." Jason took her hand and, without actually bowing over it, managed to make it a deferential gesture. "I would like to introduce my wife, Lynne."

Lynne could feel the intensity of the older woman's scrutiny as the dark, secretive eyes burned into her.

"Come and sit down. My husband will join us presently. Ah, here he is now."

Matteo D'Allasio was as different as his wife from what Lynne had conjured up in her imagination. He was tall and heavily built, but with an athletic grace; the gray in his carefully cut hair did not age him, but rather added a special touch of elegance.

Drinks and small biscuits were passed and Signora D'Allasio said, "I am sorry not to entertain you in a more festive manner, but, as you see, we are in mourning."

"Oh, of course," Lynne murmured. "I am so very sorry. It was a great tragedy."

"Your husband's loss, too, was an unhappy one," Matteo said. "How fortunate that your wedding tour included Firenze."

"The marriage was rather sudden, I believe." Isabella's tone made the words sound almost insolent.

"Not at all," Jason said smoothly. "It was postponed because of my brother's death, and because of that it was a very quiet ceremony."

"You did not mention it in Madrid," Isabella persisted.

"It hardly seemed the time for such an announcement," he said stiffly.

"Did Tonio know we were coming? May we see him soon?" Lynne asked.

Isabella tugged a bell rope and, when the maid appeared, she sent her to bring Tonio.

He arrived with laggard footsteps, but after coming a little way into the room, he caught sight of Lynne. He stopped dead still, his face suddenly transformed with a flush of joy, and hurled himself pell mell into her waiting arms. He buried his face against her and then she was on her knees beside him.

"I missed you so," she said softly in Italian.

"I didn't think I'd ever see you again."

"Didn't they tell you your Uncle Jason and I were coming?"

"They only said my Uncle Jason was bringing his new wife. I was afraid it was the lady from the circus."

Lynne gasped.

"What's this?" Matteo demanded. He looked accusingly at Jason. "My grandson says he thought you were married to someone from a circus. What does the boy mean?"

99

Jason looked completely baffled.

"It was just a misunderstanding on Tonio's part," Lynne put in hastily. "You know how small children can get an idea into their heads."

"But what on earth would lead him to believe his uncle had married a circus performer?"

Lynne hesitated but all three adults were staring at her. "It's really just nonsense. A woman who was a visitor of—at Longridge wore rather a lot of eye makeup, green eyeliner and shadow. Tonio said he had seen a clown with the same kind of eyes and got it into his head that the lady was a circus performer, too. I told you—it was nothing."

She stole a glance at Jason. He seemed to be struggling between annoyance and laughter.

Very softly to Tonio she said, "Zio Jason would like a hug from you."

Tonio untwined his arms from Lynne's neck and obediently climbed onto Jason's lap. "Are you and Lynne going to stay with us? Please, Zio Jason?"

As Jason, of course, could not understand the child's Italian words and the D'Allasios were apparently not going to translate his invitation, Lynne said, "Oh, how sweet, Jason. Tonio wants us to stay here and visit. That was what he said, wasn't it?" she appealed innocently to his grandparents. She was being careful that when she spoke Italian it was slowly and in simple words. Then to Tonio, she said, "I'm afraid not, *carissimo,* but we are going to stay on in Firenze and see the beautiful sights. We hope your grandparents will let you have dinner with us tomorrow. Would you like that, Tonio?"

"Oh, yes. Please may I, *Nonna?*" he cried eagerly.

"We will see," his grandmother said. "Now run along and have your supper."

He kissed them both good-bye. "I'm glad you're my aunt now," he told Lynne.

At a signal from Jason, Lynne rose. "We must be going, too. Thank you so much for letting us come."

"What time may we pick Tonio up tomorrow?" Jason asked. "We can give him an early meal so he will get to bed on time."

The two D'Allasios exchanged glances and then agreed on a time. "We wouldn't hear of your bringing him all the way back out to the villa. We'll send someone for him."

Just as they reached the door, a broad-shouldered, squat little man entered.

"Signor and Signora Corey, this is my cousin, Vincente Guardino."

He turned baleful eyes upon them and muttered an Italian greeting.

"Thank you again," Lynne said to Isabella. "And don't worry. We'll take very good care of Tonio."

In the car she turned to Jason. "Well, did you think it was a successful beginning?"

"With Tonio, yes. It couldn't have been more so."

"But not with his grandparents?"

He was silent for a minute. Then he said, "Did you notice the way their faces show no expression?"

She shivered a little. "As if they were carved from ice."

"There was one moment they did show something. When Tonio came in and threw himself into your arms. They looked murderous."

Murderous—they looked murderous. It was only an expression, but it made her feel colder than ever. "I didn't like the looks of that Cousin Vincente much, did you?"

"In every country there are some people who look

on all foreigners with distrust. Maybe that's what was wrong with Vincente. On the other hand, maybe it was personal."

Somehow, though she told herself it was all foolishness, Lynne felt afraid. There was something about the D'Allasios that disturbed her, besides the chilliness of their manner. They were so different from what she had expected, so much younger and more stylish. She had pictured them as an elderly, doddering couple who would have difficulty keeping up with a lively grandson. Where had she gotten that idea? Had Madelaine planted it in her mind?

The concierge had mentioned that they could have breakfast in their rooms or, if it was a fine day, on the roof terrace.

Jason had turned to Lynne and she said, "Oh, on the roof, please."

Now they were sitting in the tiny roof garden, consuming rolls and jam and coffee and looking out at the superb view of Florence.

"I didn't realize how close the hotel is to the duomo," Lynne said. "I think I'll visit it this morning, if you don't, mind. Perhaps you have business calls to make to London."

"Yes, I should talk to the office today."

The roof garden was enclosed on two sides by walls which probably formed a useful windbreak. The tables and chairs were wrought-iron painted white, and there were gay window boxes of flowers beside the railing.

"They serve drinks up here in the late afternoon. Do you think Tonio would enjoy coming up for a lemonade while we have an apéritif before we go to the restaurant?" Jason asked.

"That's a good idea. It's not easy for a child that

age to sit in one place for too long. Coming here first will break up the evening for him."

After they finished breakfast, Lynne got out the guide book and set off for the Piazza del Duomo. The cathedral with its campanile and baptistry had a strange appeal for her. They were not as magnificent, perhaps, as others she had seen, but the strong design of dark green and white marble gave them a fresh, clean look which she liked. The great domed ediface was so different from the ornately carved Gothic cathedral at Milan. She had never seen dark green marble used with white in quite this way.

She spent a long time rapt with admiration, studying the world renowned door panels of Ghiberti's; they were truly masterpieces.

She was so immersed in the visual sensations she was experiencing that she felt particularly vulnerable and, as lunchtime approached, she thought she could not bear to sit making polite, meaningless conversation with Jason. To be with him and not share openly all she was feeling and thinking would be a refined torture when she was so moved by the ancient beauty of her surroundings, and yet she dared not be totally open with him for fear some of her feelings for him would spill over. She decided to take the cowardly way out and phoned the hotel to leave a message for him that she was going to visit the Uffizi Gallery and would return in midafternoon.

The Botticellis, Ghirlandaios, and Da Vincis were good therapy and, by the time she returned to the hotel, she felt transported beyond her own private troubles.

She changed into the rust wool suit and knocked on Jason's door to tell him she was ready to leave for the villa to pick up Tonio.

"Did you enjoy your sightseeing?" he inquired in a tight voice.

"Very much. I could stay in Florence for a year, I think."

Yesterday on the drive to the D'Allasio villa she had been too nervous to enjoy the scenery to the full. Today, already drunk with beauty, she was totally receptive to her surroundings.

"Whenever I think of Florence," she said, musingly, as they drove, "I'll see in my mind the cypresses like black candle flames, reaching toward heaven."

The evening with Tonio was enchanting. He was delighted with the roof garden, as she had known he would be, and Jason had chosen a restaurant with tables outdoors overhanging the Arno.

At that early hour there were hardly any other patrons in the restaurant and the waiter made a big fuss over Tonio, pretending to mistake him for the head of the family and consulting him about whether each dish was just right.

It was a merry evening and toward the end Lynne said, "You should begin to learn English, Tonio, so you can talk with Zio Jason."

Tonio clapped his hands. "Oh, I'd like that. Let's begin now!"

"Well, the way we say *prego* is 'please' and *grazie* is 'thank you.' Those are always good to begin with."

On the way back to the hotel she pointed to various things they passed and gave him the English word.

When they were almost there Jason said, "Tell Tonio we'll see him tomorrow. I tried to arrange dinner with his grandparents, but they said they don't go out in the evening since Francesca died; however, with some urging they agreed to come to a luncheon party."

She translated for Tonio the part about having

lunch together and he said, "Lynne, what is the English for *bene?*"

"It's 'good,'" she said.

He turned to Jason with a bright smile and said in careful English, "Good. Thank you, Uncle Jason."

Lynne laughed and hugged him. She wished he could be with them all the time. Everything was so much more natural and easy between her and Jason with Tonio around. She could busy herself with the boy and forget the ache in her heart.

CHAPTER NINE

The luncheon party lacked the spontaneous gaiety of the evening before. Again wearing unrelieved black, Isabella D'Allasio was as unbending as before. Matteo was no more forthcoming than she. Lynne wondered if it were hostility to herself and Jason that caused their glacial attitudes. If they were no warmer with Tonio, the poor child must be having a sad and lonely time.

Though she was glad that Tonio was part of the party, she felt constrained not to chatter fluently with him in Italian as she usually did, since Jason didn't want the D'Allasios to realize the extent of her competence in the language. So in that area, too, the party lacked sparkle.

Finally she said to Isabella, "I have been enthralled with your magnificent art galleries, but one thing I want to do before we leave Florence is to visit the Boboli Gardens. It occurred to me it would make a pleasant outing for Tonio, and it would make it more enjoyable for me if he were along." Turning to the boy, she said slowly, "If your grandmother allows it, would you like to go to the Boboli Gardens tomorrow?"

As she had foreseen, he turned, pleading, to his grandmother. Lynne felt guiltily that she was being somewhat unfair in letting him know of the invitation because by doing so she was putting added pressure on his grandmother.

Isabella agreed though without enthusiasm, but then

Lynne had never seen her show enthusiasm for anything.

A little later Tonio seemed struck with a sudden idea and, turning to his grandmother he said excitedly, "Perhaps I could stay with Lynne and Zio Jason when you and Grandfather go to the Lido with Vincente and Paola and the others? I hate staying with Carolina. She's so cross."

Isabella hushed him instantly.

"Is there some way we could be of help?" Lynne asked. "Wasn't Tonio asking if he could stay with us while you go somewhere?"

"It is nothing," Isabella said. "My husband thought he might have to go to Venice on business and wanted me to go with him. However, our plans have changed and we are not going after all. It was just a mistake of Tonio's."

Matteo's eyes went instantly to hers. There was an unspoken communication between them. He seemed even more disapproving than usual, but it looked to Lynne as if Isabella's eyes were commanding him to silence.

Meanwhile Tonio was sitting crestfallen since his grandmother had quieted him. Lynne said to him, "We'll have fun tomorrow. It was kind of your grandmother to agree to let us take you to the gardens."

It seemed to cheer him a little.

As coffee was brought to the table Matteo, as if coming to a decision, asked, "And when do you plan to leave Firenze?"

It seemed as if he had thrown down a challenge.

Jason took his time answering. He stirred his coffee slowly. Finally he said, "We have made no definite plans for departure. It seems important to me to get better acquainted with my nephew, and for you to get better acquainted with us."

Matteo's lips tightened and Lynne thought she saw a flash of anger in Isabella's eyes.

The cards were on the table now. Without putting it in so many words, Jason had let them understand that he was not giving up on his wish to have Tonio. They were obviously not pleased.

When they had left to return to the villa, Jason said quietly, "I'm going to call Darren and ask him to come. The D'Allasios will never give up Tonio voluntarily, that's obvious. We've given them plenty of opportunity to see that Tonio enjoys being with us and that we would be responsible, caring guardians. But they're as hostile to the idea as ever. I can see that. It's time to begin legal steps."

Lynne nodded in unhappy agreement. "Jason, there was one slightly odd thing. When Tonio asked his grandmother if he could stay with us, he said, 'When you and Grandfather go to the Lido with Vincente and Paola and the others.' But when I questioned her, pretending I hadn't quite understood, Isabella's translation was that Matteo had wanted her to go on a business trip to Venice but it had been cancelled. And then Matteo looked at her as if that was the first he knew of its being cancelled, and I could swear she was practically ordering him not to speak of it. Why would Tonio say the Lido and she change it to Venice?"

"The Lido is an island in the Adriatic just a few minutes by boat from Venice. Perhaps Matteo's business was in Venice but they were planning to stay on the Lido. It's a fashionable resort."

He seemed to be thinking aloud. "There's a gambling casino there, and the International Film Festival is held there. It seems odd they'd be going on a business trip with a group of other people."

"And I'm sure she only made up her mind to cancel it because of us. She didn't want Tonio with us while they were away from Florence. I could be misinterpreting but I'm certain that's it. Another thing Tonio said was, 'I hate staying with Carolina. She's so cross,' which certainly implies they've left him with her before—though I suppose it wouldn't necessarily have been for any length of time. It could have been just for a day or an evening, but it sounded as if they've gone away overnight and left him before, which seems at odds with what they told us about not going anywhere because of being in mourning."

"Yes, it is strange," Jason said. "I will be surprised if they let Tonio come to us tomorrow after all, considering the way our interview ended today."

Nevertheless, Jason's prediction proved groundless. Tonio was delivered to the hotel in time for lunch as had been promised. They were to return him to the villa in time for his early supper.

They went to a nearby *trattoria* for lunch and had a hilarious time teaching Tonio the English words for water, knife, fork, spoon, and so on, while Tonio insisted that at the same time Jason must learn the Italian equivalents. Whenever Lynne had to correct his uncle's pronunciation, Tonio found it uproariously funny.

When lunch was over, Jason asked, "Do you think you two could amuse yourselves for half an hour before we start for the Boboli Gardens? I have to make some calls to London, but I'll meet you in the lobby in thirty minutes."

"Of course," Lynne said. "Come, Tonio. Would you like to walk across the Ponte Vecchio?"

He slipped his hand into hers and they set off. In

the center of the bridge they paused so that Tonio could look down at the water, and then began to leisurely window-shop their way back. Lynne found the window displays charming, but she hadn't yet been into any of the small shops that lined the bridge.

"Oh, look," Tonio cried at one window, pointing to a group of cunningly crafted metal animals. "See the funny giraffe with the green eyes!"

Lynne admired them and then her eye was caught by a gilt pendant on a chain. It was a personified sun disk with swirling rays and a smiling face.

"What are you looking at, Zia Lynne?" Tonio asked.

She pointed. "That necklace. It's supposed to be the sun's face and he's smiling. Wouldn't that be lucky, to have a sun to always shine on you?"

"Why don't you buy it?"

"Oh, no," she said and started to move on, but he held fast to her hand. "It would look nice on your blue pullover."

She hesitated. She had never thought of buying anything for herself on this trip because Jason had bought her so much—more than she needed by far. But it would be fun to have one piece of costume jewelry as a kind of good luck charm. Impulsively she went into the shop and asked to see the pendant. As the shopkeeper put it into her hands, she saw that the workmanship was even lovelier than it had looked at a distance.

"How much is it?" she asked.

The shopkeeper named the price and at first Lynne thought she had heard him wrong, but he repeated it as she once more translated the lire into pounds. It was impossible! But then suddenly she understood and felt like a naive idiot. The beautiful sun pendant lying so heavy in her hand was real gold. She should have realized. The goldsmiths of Florence were world famous for their craftsmanship. Somehow it had not occurred to her that such whimsical pieces as the little animals and this sun disk would be fashioned of real gold.

"I'm sorry. It's lovely, but it's too expensive." She gave him an embarrassed smile and handed it back.

"Why didn't you buy it, Lynne?" Tonio demanded.

"Because your Aunt Lynne is very foolish," she said when they were outside the shop again. "I assumed it was only gilt but it's real gold and cost far too much."

"But isn't Zio Jason rich?" he asked innocently.

She looked down at him, "Well, that has nothing to do with it. Just having money doesn't mean one should spend it foolishly on things one doesn't need."

Jason was waiting in the lobby when they returned to the hotel. They crossed the river, going back across the Ponte Vecchio, this time Tonio holding Jason's hand. At one point Lynne realized they were dropping behind and turned back. "I want to show Uncle Jason the giraffe, Lynne," Tonio called. She nodded and smiled and waited until they caught up.

They walked around the Pitti Palace, deciding Tonio would rather go on to the gardens than go in to see any of the paintings.

Shortly beyond the Pitti Palace they came upon a *gelato* vendor and Tonio asked if he could have one. Lynne groaned. "Tonio, how could you after that enormous lunch?"

"Is it too expensive, Lynne?" he asked anxiously. "Even though Uncle Jason's rich, would it be spending his money foolishly?"

She burst out laughing. "No, of course not. There's a difference between buying an ice and buying a gold necklace. I only meant I thought you might burst if you ate one more thing."

"Oh, no." He was very serious. "I won't burst. I always have room for an ice. They hardly take up any space at all."

"Then run and get one." She smiled.

Sometimes during lengthy exchanges in Italian between Lynne and Tonio, Jason assumed a look of frustration at being left out. "What was that all about?" he asked.

"It loses a lot in translation," she said lightly, but seeing he was still waiting, she had to go on. The real explanation went back to the story of the golden sun disk and she certainly wasn't going to tell him about that, so she merely said, "When he asked for an ice, I was somewhat dismayed after that big lunch he ate. So he asked if it would be too expensive, and I said you could afford it but that I was afraid he would burst. However, he said a *gelato* didn't take up much room and he always had space enough for one."

Jason seemed satisfied with this abbreviated version of the story, and while Tonio happily consumed his *gelato*, they admired the lovely views of the city from the Giardino del Cavaliere. They roamed about the gardens and the Buontalenti Grotto, and as they turned into the Viottolone, Lynne stopped transfixed.

How very Italian it was, the very essence of the Italian style—formalized and yet with a kind of spacious and expansive joy and appreciation of beauty and heritage. Down either side of the wide avenue ran a row of the incomparable dark cypress trees. The Viottolone stretched on and on, and set into the trees every few yards was a marble statue. Some were ancient, some medieval, and while none perhaps were absolute masterpieces, each was lovely and special in its own way.

With the energy that only a five year old could possess, Tonio began to run down the avenue, zigzagging back and forth across it to touch each statue.

"Look at the face on this one, Lynne," Jason said. "You can almost see what she's thinking."

"It's incredible, isn't it?" Lynne said. "A country so rich in art that they can put all these marvelous pieces out in the open in public gardens for the people to enjoy."

At the end of the avenue of cypresses they came to the Piazzale dell'Isolotto. The small island in the round pool was all planted with flowers and citrus trees and in the center was a graceful fountain. Around the pool was a circular path with benches set here and there, and dense planting enclosed the whole area to compose a spot of green serenity.

"Here are two new words for you, Tonio," Lynne said. "Island and fountain." She explained the meaning of each and then Tonio said, "Now it's Zio Jason's turn," and obediently Jason repeated after her, *"isola, fontana."*

After circling the island twice, Lynne and Jason sat down on a bench. A sweet-faced woman holding a baby was sitting there, her older son playing nearby. Immediately Tonio and the other boy engaged in a game of tag, and then a wild chase around the path to the far side of the island.

The woman smiled at Lynne and said, "You have a fine son. He looks very much like his father."

"Oh, do you think so? My—my husband will be so pleased. Actually Tonio is our nephew." She repeated what the woman had said to Jason and he looked so proud that something twisted in Lynne's heart. For a little while it had seemed as if they were truly what they seemed to be, a real family on a pleasant outing. It was so easy to forget, or almost to forget, just for a few minutes, that it was all make-believe—that Tonio, and Jason, would never really be hers.

To distract herself Lynne asked, "May I hold the baby? He's such a beautiful child."

His mother gave him a kiss and put him in Lynne's arms. "That's very nice. It will give me a chance to have a cigarette." She opened her bag and took out a cigarette case.

"That is the most exquisite purse," Lynne said enthusiastically. "And the matching cigarette case. I've always heard that Florentine leatherwork was the finest in the world. Now I can believe it."

The woman seemed pleased. "These are from my husband's shop, just off the Piazza del Duomo."

"Then it's near our hotel. Perhaps I'll be able to visit it."

"I'll give you his card with the address. If you go there, you must tell him I said he was to give you a good price."

Lynne laughed and, as she was holding the baby with both arms, asked Jason to put the card in her purse.

They sat for a while longer and then the woman looked at her watch. "Oh, dear, it's half-past four. I must leave. Giorgio!" she called to her son. "Time to go home."

Reluctantly the two boys parted and Lynne handed the baby back to his mother.

"Good-bye. I won't forget to visit your husband's shop," Lynne said.

After a bit Jason said, "I suppose we should be getting back to the hotel, too, and get the car to take

Tonio home. It's so peaceful here, I hate to move. I'm afraid it will be our last outing with Tonio—for a while."

Perhaps it was only that the afternoon was wearing itself away, but suddenly Lynne felt cold.

As they started up the Viottolone Tonio said, "Let's play hide-and-seek. This is a good place for that game. You hide, Lynne. We'll close our eyes, and I'll count to twenty out loud. It will be a good Italian lesson for Zio Jason, learning to count."

She explained to Jason and, laughing, he agreed.

She positioned herself behind one of the statues and before long an excited Tonio triumphantly pounced on her.

"Oh, is that Lynne?" Jason said. "I saw her posed there quietly, but I thought it was one of the marble nymphs. I suppose I should have wondered why a marble nymph would be wearing a blue pullover."

She translated for Tonio, who went into gales of laughter. "I know a new word for him, Lynne. Teach him 'hiding-place.'"

"Tonio says you must learn the word for 'hiding-place,' Jason. That's *nascondiglio*."

Tonio was still laughing as Jason haltingly repeated the word. Then he cried, "Now I'm it. Hide your eyes." They heard his scampering footsteps as he dashed off as they stood with their eyes closed.

At first Lynne didn't look too closely behind each nearby statue as she didn't want to spoil his fun by finding him too quickly, but after a few minutes she looked more carefully and still didn't see him. She went over to Jason, thinking perhaps he had spotted the boy and from the same motive as hers had pretended not to see him.

"Have you found him?"

He shook his head. "He's not over on this side."

They hurried on, but he had vanished.

The game had gone on too long. "Tonio!" Lynne called loudly. "Tonio. Come back. We give up." But along the wide avenue, no small figure stepped out from a hiding place.

"Perhaps he went back to the area near the island," Jason said. "You stay here." But he returned quickly, shaking his head. "I'll search behind the row of cypresses. Keep calling his name."

"I'll stay here in the path so he can see me if he comes out of hiding," she said. She walked rapidly up and down the avenue shouting his name. She could hear Jason's voice calling, too. Then she saw him cross to look behind the trees on the other side.

Icy fear was beginning to numb her. It was impossible that a small boy could vanish so quickly in the middle of a joyous game on a sunny afternoon, she told herself, but the panic didn't subside.

Jason reappeared, his face gaunt. "No sign of him."

"I'm going for a policeman." Lynne heard herself saying the words before she knew she was going to utter them.

"But he must just be hiding!" Jason said.

Lynne swallowed hard and shook her head. "I don't think so. He would know we're frightened. When we played hide-and-seek at Longridge, I explained he must never keep hidden if I said the game was over, because I might be too alarmed and run around looking in a panic and get hurt. He'd remember that. You stay where he can see you if he comes out into the avenue, but I'm going for the police.

"I'm afraid, Jason. I'm afraid."

CHAPTER TEN

She sped along the avenue, out of the garden and into a main street. Almost immediately, she saw a police van and uttered a prayer of thanks.

"Please help me," she gasped, out of breath from running. "My nephew is lost in the Boboli Gardens."

To her annoyance, the young police officer opened his log book and began to make notes. "Your name, please."

She wanted to scream at him that her name was of no importance, but a moment's reflection told her that arguing would only waste time, so she gave him the information he asked for. Then he let her tell him her story. "My husband and I were on an outing in the Boboli Gardens with my nephew, Tonio. He's five years old. Just before we started back to the hotel, Tonio suggested a game of hide-and-seek. We closed our eyes for a moment and when we looked for him, he had vanished. My husband ran back to the Piazzale dell'Isolotto and he looked behind the cypresses, but I stayed out in the middle of the Viottolone so he could see me if he came out of hiding. We called and called, but he didn't answer. Something terrible has happened."

"It shouldn't be hard for a small boy to stay hidden for a while in the Boboli Gardens," the policeman said with maddening calm.

"But he wouldn't," Lynne said firmly. "I know him too well to believe that. We had an understanding about never frightening each other that way."

"Suppose he wanted to frighten you, to punish you for something. Perhaps you had had some disagreement this afternoon."

"No!" Lynne was furious now. "There was no disagreement. It had been a perfect afternoon. Nothing had gone wrong between us. I tell you—something's happened to him."

"Very well, Signora. We will look into it." He added more kindly, "Don't worry. Small boys manage to lose themselves every day."

She tried to smile but without much success.

She returned to Jason with three policemen. She had been hoping against hope that when she returned Tonio would be with him, but when she saw him standing alone her heart sank.

The men asked to see the exact spot where he had disappeared. Two of the policemen set out searching while the other questioned them again.

"What would he do if he found himself lost?"

"He'd come back onto the Viottolone," Lynne said. "He'd call to us."

"But suppose he confused the direction and wandered the wrong way and got too far for you to hear each other. Suppose someone found him lost and alone. What would he do?"

"He'd ask them to bring him to the Viottolone near the island," she replied promptly.

"But if they tried that and couldn't see you because you were searching for him—"

"I told you," Lynne said impatiently, "one of us has been in plain sight right here in the avenue at all times for that very reason."

"Very well. Then suppose someone found him and asked where he lived. Does he know the name of your hotel?"

Lynne thought carefully. "I'm not sure. I think

he does, but if he were frightened he might have forgotten. However he lives at present with his grandparents in their villa between Firenze and Fiesole. I suppose he could have told them that."

"Very well. The others will stay and search. We will telephone the hotel and his grandparents to see if there is any word." He called the others over and asked Lynne to give them a full description of the boy.

She approximated his height and weight and as she described his little yellow shirt and short brown trousers, her voice broke.

She found that Jason was gripping her hand hard. She knew what a torment it must be for him not to understand what was being said. She could feel the tension in him, and she was grateful for his trust in her, letting her get on with it, without interrupting and demanding explanations. Only a very controlled man could manage that, she thought, and from somewhere in her memory a sentence floated to the surface of her mind: A good executive is one who knows how to delegate authority.

The phone call to the hotel produced nothing. There had been no word for Signor or Signora Corey.

Next the young police officer called the D'Allasios' number and asked to speak to Signor D'Allasio. Lynne heard him explaining that Tonio had gotten separated from his aunt and uncle, and they wanted to know if the Signore had had any news."

"Yes, yes, I see. Very well." He turned to Lynne. "The boy is at home, safe and well."

"Jason," she cried. "He's all right. He's back at home. Safe!"

She found herself in his arms, grateful for the strength of his shoulder as she leaned against him.

She heard his exclamation of relief, too, and then

almost immediately his commanding executive's voice sliced into her joy. "Ask how and when he returned."

She turned and repeated the question and the police officer spoke into the phone again. Then he said to Lynne, "A cousin found him wandering in the gardens, apparently abandoned, crying. He searched but there was no sight of you anywhere so eventually he took him home. They arrived half an hour ago."

"That's nonsense," she began, but then turned back to Jason and repeated the story.

He looked at his watch. "You can see that that is impossible. Have the officer make a note of the time."

Lynne did so. When he had hung up the phone, she said, "Something is wrong with their story. This is very important, officer. I request that you come with us to the D'Allasios' home. I want to be sure the boy is safe, and I want it proved who is lying."

She could see that he was reluctant, but she remained adamant. "If I must sign a formal request, tell me how to go about it."

He looked into her earnest face for a moment and then softened. "Very well. We will call on the D'Allasios to make certain the boy is really safe."

Two policemen rode in the front of the car, Lynne and Jason in the back seat. She was conscious of Jason's arm against hers as they rode side by side to the villa. She felt a fleeting embarrassment as she remembered throwing herself into his arms when they heard that Tonio was safe. But then she decided it was nothing to be ashamed of. It had not been a lover's embrace. It was only two people clinging together in relief when an emergency was over. There was nothing personal about it.

The maid who answered the door looked alarmed

when she saw the police, but she asked haughtily, "Who shall I say is calling?"

"Police officers Siempe and Torella, and Signor and Signora Corey. We require to see Signor and Signora D'Allasio."

She returned a few minutes later and led them to a sitting room. The group of people were as still as if posed for a tableau, the D'Allasios, Vincente Guardino, an older man, and a young woman.

"Yes?" Matteo D'Allasio looked directly at Officer Siempe, ignoring Jason and Lynne.

"We have a few questions to ask about your grandson."

"It was by the grace of God my cousin found him," Isabella said. "I will never forgive these people for their carelessness. Or myself for allowing Tonio to go out in their company."

"That does not answer anything, Signora," the officer said. "Exactly how was he found and brought home?"

Vincente spoke up. "I had been in town on business. I had some free time before an appointment so, since it was a fine afternoon, I decided to stroll in the Boboli Gardens. While I was walking along I heard a whimpering sound. I thought it might be an injured dog, so I went off the path and discovered it was a child. I picked him up and imagine my surprise to see it was my cousin's grandson!

"I asked him what he was doing there and he said his aunt and uncle had brought him to the gardens. He said they had suggested playing hide-and-seek. They hid and he found them once behind a statue kissing. Then they told him this time he must close his eyes and count to one hundred. When he had finished counting, they were gone."

Lynne felt enflamed with a fury she had never known. It was one of the hardest things she had ever done to hold her tongue and let him continue with his lies.

"The poor child had looked and looked for them, wandering around, crying and calling their names, but they had vanished."

"So what did you do?" the police officer asked.

"I searched for them for, oh, twenty minutes or so, but then"—he shrugged suggestively—"I thought, well, after all they are newlyweds and they apparently wanted some privacy. Who knew where they were and what they were doing? Maybe it was better if we didn't stumble upon them. Or perhaps they were so engrossed in each other that they had forgotten all about the boy and returned to the hotel." The little man's eyes glittered maliciously.

Through a red rage Lynne knew she would like to have killed him. She was only grateful that Jason didn't understand because he might well have done so.

"The boy was growing more hysterical so I brought him home."

"And what time did you arrive?"

"A bit after five."

"Do you confirm that?" the officer asked the D'Allasios.

They nodded. "It was about ten minutes after five, perhaps a quarter past. Our friends were here drinking coffee. They can confirm it also."

The other policeman was making notes as Vincente spoke. Officer Siempe turned to Lynne with a question in his eyes.

"The time they returned may be correct, but every other word is a vicious lie," she said in a tight, furious voice. "At four thirty we were still sitting beside the island. A few minutes later we started home and Tonio suggested a game of hide-and-seek. I hid and he found me. Then he hid and he just—vanished. When we couldn't find him, I went for the police—within ten minutes.

"Our game hadn't started until after four thirty. Tonio hadn't disappeared before a quarter to five, and yet he arrived here at a quarter past. But it takes nearly half an hour to drive from there to this villa. So how could Tonio possibly have wandered around looking for us? How could Vincente have searched for another twenty minutes? There simply wasn't time. Vincente would have to have started back with Tonio immediately after he disappeared."

The D'Allasios were staring at her angrily as they realized for the first time that she spoke fluent Italian. However, there was a crafty note of triumph in Matteo's voice as he said, "Ah, but we have only your word for the time Tonio vanished. I submit that it was earlier, much earlier. Naturally when you finally realized he was gone and went to find a policeman, you wouldn't want to admit you had carelessly misplaced him hours before."

"It was after four thirty when he disappeared," Lynne's words rang out clearly.

Matteo smiled. It was not a pleasant smile. "But can you prove it?" he asked.

"Yes, I can prove it. At four thirty we were sitting on a bench beside the pool at the Piazzale dell'Isolotto. We were talking to a woman who was there with her children. Tonio and her son were playing."

"And you can find this woman again, Signora?" Isabella asked slyly.

"I can find her." She opened her purse, took out

the card, and handed it to the officer. "She is the wife of the man who owns this shop. She will remember us."

The D'Allasios were clearly taken aback. But Matteo said with a sneer, "And she will remember the time, no doubt?"

"Yes," Lynne said confidently. "She looked at her watch and said it was four thirty—time for her to start home."

For the first time the D'Allasios looked uneasy.

"I think we had better see the boy," Officer Siempe said.

"No!" Isabella's voice was sharp. "He has been put to bed. He went through a terrible experience. He was hysterical when he arrived home. He's only a baby. I can't have him disturbed. It's impossible."

"Under ordinary circumstances I would respect your wishes regarding your grandson, but someone has lied to the police. That is a serious matter. We will check Signora Corey's story. Meanwhile we will see the boy," the police officer said firmly.

Isabella stared frozen-faced at him, and then, seeing his determination, started to rise.

"No." He stopped her. "Send the maid to fetch him."

A few moments later Tonio appeared on the threshhold, his face red and blotchy from weeping. When he saw Jason and Lynne, he gave a glad cry and, detaching himself from the maid's hand, flung himself at Lynne.

"I'm so sorry," he cried. "I knew you'd be frightened. I didn't mean to, Lynne. Honestly I didn't."

"Of course you didn't, darling. I knew you wouldn't. Can you tell us what happened?"

"From the beginning, little one," the police officer said.

Tonio was puzzled. "When was the beginning?"

"Remember Giorgio who played with you at the Piazzale dell'Isolotto?" Lynne suggested. "And then his mother called to him that it was time to go. Begin there. That was at four thirty, Officer, as the woman in the park will confirm."

"A few minutes after Giorgio left, you said we must go, too," Tonio said. "And when we went out on the avenue, I said let's play hide-and-seek. You hid behind a statue and I found you. Then I hid behind a cypress tree. Then I saw Cousin Vincente. He put his finger to his lips—like this." Tonio demonstrated. "Then he said that place was too easy. He said he'd show me a better one. He picked me up and started to carry me. I thought we were getting too far away and I tried to tell him, but he put his hand over my mouth and ran to his car. Then he started to drive home. I told him that wasn't the way to play. I said you'd be scared and you'd taught me never to scare who you're playing with because that's not a good game. But he wouldn't listen. And neither would Grandmother and Grandfather. They told Carolina to put me to bed."

He started to cry again and Lynne comforted him. "It's all right, darling. We were scared, but we knew it wasn't your fault. And now that we know you're safe, we aren't scared anymore." The last words were flung out as a challenge.

"I think that will be all," the officer said. "I will, of course, make a complete report of this to my superiors."

Lynne gave Tonio a hug and whispered, "We'll see you as soon as we can." They swept from the room, feeling the malevolent eyes of the five adults behind them boring into their backs.

In the car Lynne said to Jason, "That dear, brave

little boy. He told the truth despite them all." She recounted Tonio's story of how Vincente had spirited him away.

"I'll settle with that man one day," Jason said grimly, and then was silent on the way back to the hotel.

The police car let them out in front of their hotel. "I can't thank you enough, Officers," said Lynne. "You were very helpful. It's a complicated situation. I think your help today may have gone a long way toward resolving it satisfactorily."

"I'm glad it turned out well, Signora," Officer Siempe said. "He's a fine boy."

When the police car pulled away, Jason turned to Lynne and gripped her hands. "Thank God for you, Lynne." His voice was fervent. "Thank God for your good judgment in going for the police immediately. Thank God for your courage in standing up to all of them."

Her heart constricted. "It was you who realized the significance of the timing, Jason."

"But you were the one who could communicate with them and get to the truth of the matter. I'm not accustomed to standing by and watching someone do my work for me. But I watched you take them all on with such confidence in your face—I knew it would be all right."

"That just shows you're a good executive. You know how to hire a person with the right requisites for the job."

"Hire someone?" He looked disturbed, but before he could say more a familiar voice behind them called out, "Well, it's about time you two showed up! I've been hanging about for two hours."

They whirled around. "Darren!" Jason went forward and clapped Darren Lloyd on both shoulders.

Then he caught hold of Lynne's arm and pulled her over. "Lynne, I owe you the best dinner in all Florence, but would you settle for the first *trattoria* we stumble across where we won't have to change our clothes to eat? I've got to catch this legal type up on what's been happening."

"Of course," Lynne said, "but maybe you two would like to talk business alone."

"Alone?" He seemed bewildered. "You're the heroine of the whole piece. Besides, there's a lot that happened today that we haven't really thrashed out."

"Come along, my girl," Darren said. "I haven't seen you since the wedding, and that's a good deal too long."

Wedding, Lynne thought. It seemed as if she had lived through several lifetimes since then.

When they were seated in a quiet corner in a little *trattoria*, with a bottle of red wine on the table in front of them and orders of *gnocchi verde* on the way, Jason said, "To cover the preliminaries briefly, for the first couple of days everything between us and the D'Allasios was very polite, very civilized. Not warm, but civilized. Of course with Tonio, it was a different story. Lynne had made a real conquest there." He flashed her a brief smile.

"Then yesterday we entertained the three of them at lunch. Toward the end Matteo asked when we were leaving Florence. I decided it was time we put the cards on the table and said our stay was indefinite—that we wanted to see more of Tonio. You could practically see their hackles rise. Earlier they had promised that Tonio could spend this afternoon with us in the Boboli Gardens. After the gauntlet was thrown down, I never expected they would let him come, but they showed up with him right on time. The kicker was, late in the afternoon he was abducted by Isabella's cousin, Vincente Guardino—a nasty customer if ever I saw one."

"Abducted!" Darren was startled.

They recounted the whole sequence of events, step by step.

By now their food had arrived and, to her astonishment, Lynne found that she was ravenously hungry.

"So you see," Jason said, his fork halfway to his mouth, "they obviously hoped to discredit us completely. They knew we'd eventually have to go to the police or get in touch with them, and they had witnesses there ready to swear that Vincente had brought home the hysterical child we'd abandoned—or carelessly misplaced. What they didn't count on was that Lynne would move so fast to get the police in on it immediately and be able to establish the times so precisely that their story was obviously nonsense. You should have seen her take charge!"

His eyes shone with pride and Lynne felt herself flushing. "That was all because of Jason's precaution in warning me not to let them realize that I spoke Italian very well," she said. "I suppose it didn't occur to them that we could alert the police to the problem so quickly and be able to communicate about exactly what was going on. And they certainly couldn't have guessed that we'd meet that nice woman in the park who could establish the time. Actually that was the merest stroke of luck."

"Luck and your friendly nature and command of the language," Jason said.

"What I don't see," Darren said, "is how they could know Vincente would have a chance to snatch the boy."

"Well, of course it was only a chance, but if it hadn't worked out, they would have been no worse off than before. Perhaps he had something planned to distract us on our way home so he could grab Tonio then."

"Perhaps," Lynne said, "but I've been thinking. I wonder if the idea of hide-and-seek might not have been planted in Tonio's mind ahead of time. What he said was, 'Let's play hide-and-seek. This is a good place for that game.' Perhaps one of them had suggested to him that it was a good place to play it and he was just responding on cue."

"That could be," Darren said. "The sooner we get him away from those fiends the better. They sound like real rotters, worse even than I expected."

"Well, the police have a record of the whole affair. That should help, shouldn't it?"

"I would certainly think so. After this episode, their credit should be nil as far as the custody suit is concerned. It ought to be smooth sailing from here on."

Suddenly Lynne snapped her fingers. "Paola Malina! That's who that woman was at the D'Allisios' tonight. I had the nagging feeling she looked familiar, but there was so much else on my mind I didn't really think about it."

"Paola Malina?" Jason looked puzzled.

"Don't you remember? It was all over the press last year. She's some sort of film actress. She was in England making a film and some MP's wife shot her husband because he was having an affair with the woman. It was a big scandal at the time."

"I remember the case," Darren said.

"Paola. Where have I heard that name recently?" Jason mused.

"It was yesterday at lunch. Tonio asked his grandmother if he could stay with us while they went to the Lido with Vincente and Paola and the others. And that was another odd thing, Darren. When I pretended I didn't quite understand, she translated it differently and said she and Matteo had planned a business trip to Venice but it had been canceled."

"Matteo seemed surprised and Isabella looked daggers at him," Jason added. "We figured she had decided they shouldn't leave Tonio alone with the maid while we were on the scene."

"The whole thing didn't jibe with the way they told us they didn't go out anywhere since they were in mourning."

Darren and Jason exchanged a long look which Lynne didn't understand.

"Well, old son," Darren said, "I'll start the legal wheels turning. Meanwhile, there's nothing you can do but relax and enjoy the honeymoon."

Lynne felt a peculiar combination of heartsickness and outrage at the comment, but Darren continued blandly, "Go to the museums and churches. Be seen appreciating the glories of Florence. You have an image to protect, you know—that of a devoted young couple who would make excellent guardians for a five-year-old child. You never know who may be watching."

She dropped her gaze to her plate. Today in the emergency she had been able to lay aside her personal feelings. But tomorrow how would she have the strength to keep up the charade?

Maybe she was just so exhausted by the events of the day that obstacles seemed more insurmountable than they really were. Maybe she could find her way back to that easy, casual comradeship with Jason—tomorrow when she was rested.

At the moment all she wanted was to fall into bed.

CHAPTER ELEVEN

Lynne was grateful for Darren's presence at breakfast the next morning on the small roof garden.

"I say, that is a rather smashing view, isn't it?" Darren exclaimed. "Church and bell tower and all that. Wouldn't mind wandering over and taking a look, but that's not what Jason's paying me for, right?"

"Did you set out to make me sound like a slave driver, or did it just come out that way accidentally?" Jason inquired pleasantly.

"Oh, it was totally an accident, old boy. Wouldn't think of criticizing you, especially when I remember you told Lynne you owed her the best dinner in town. I suppose you'll be making good on that tonight. And since it's possible you'll want legal advice tonight, too, I wouldn't dream of saying a word to get on your bad side between now and then. No sense ruining the chance of an invitation to a first-rate dinner. Tact is my strong point. Actually that's why I went into the legal profession. Very long on tact, if I do say so myself."

Lynne burst out laughing. "And you're subtle, too."

He looked at his watch. "Well, I'm off to start earning my fee. What are you two typical, average tourists going to do with yourselves today?"

Jason looked at Lynne. "What would you like to see?" When she hesitated, he said, "Remember, Darren's handling the legal end. There's no chance they'll let us see Tonio today, so we might as well take

Darren's advice and behave like normal tourists."

"All right. Then I'd like to go to the Academia and see Michelangelo's David. And the Monastery of St. Mark sounds interesting. Actually there's enough to do to keep busy for weeks—the Bargello Museum, the Pitti Palace, the Medici Museum."

"Let's start off with the Academia then," he said.

All the way there her mind was on Darren, wondering if everything was going well with the legal details he was handling, but once inside the Academia the genius of Michelangelo overwhelmed her thoughts and pushed everything else from her mind.

There were many fascinating pieces, but the David —well, the David was awe-inspiring. Standing alone, brilliantly lighted in a semicircular rotunda, the pure white marble figure took her breath away.

Though there were crowds of people, the statue seemed to have the same effect on all of them because there was no chattering, no shoving, only a silent group of people paying homage.

Outside afterward Jason said, "There really aren't any words for it, are there?"

She shook her head. "You know, I'm almost beginning to feel giddy. We seem to plunge from one extreme to another. Yesterday having Tonio kidnapped by that dreadful man; today viewing the sublimest of art. At the moment the idea of a nice, dull, humdrum existence sounds rather attractive. I never realized peaks and valleys could be so exhausting."

"Poor Lynne. Let's have a bit of lunch and catch our breath. Then maybe we could visit the Monastery of St. Mark. That sounds as if it might be peaceful."

Jason was right. There was a lovely collection of Fra Angelicos in the museum, so gentle, delicate, and serene. Looking at them gave Lynne a warm glow of happiness deep inside, and yet some of the children's faces reminded her of Tonio and made her want to cry at the same time.

In the cloisters, after looking at the extraordinary frescoes, they sat in the shade of an enormous cedar tree, letting the peace of the setting flow over them.

Suddenly, to her surprise, Lynne felt tears prickling at her eyes.

"Lynne! What is it?" Jason was all concern.

For a moment she couldn't speak. "I don't know," she said at last. "I think it was those sweet Fra Angelico paintings. They made me think of Tonio."

"You're not worried about him are you, Lynne? It was a despicable thing his grandparents did yesterday, but it was aimed at me, not at him. They wouldn't harm the boy, I'm sure of that. It will work out—thanks in great part to you. He'll soon be safe at home with us in England—at Longridge."

He couldn't know how his words were twisting the knife in her heart. Of course she wanted Tonio safe at Longridge. But she would miss him so, because she couldn't go there, not for the six months Jason had suggested, not for any time at all.

How could she live at Longridge, under Jason's roof, seeing him every weekend? It was too much to ask. When he looked at her with his searching gray eyes, her knees went weak. She longed for his touch. The memory of the strength of his body sent shivers through her. But he was not for her, could never be. She was a temporary convenience to him. She knew he was truly grateful for her part in yesterday's adventure, but his heart belonged to Justine. That one mad, glorious moment when he had seen her as a woman was only an isolated fragment in time. She could never be anything more to him than a loyal employee. She was a highly paid and trusted employee, but that was all. It wasn't enough, not when her heart turned over at the sight of his lithe, strong figure, the shape of his mouth. She would be bound to betray herself eventually if she were to go back to Longridge.

"Jason," she said after the lengthening silence, "you know I'll do everything I can to help you in taking Tonio home. But as for the rest, I can't go with you. You can find another tutor for him."

"Lynne, what are you talking about? You know we agreed—"

She held up a weary hand. "You won't really need me then, once the papers are signed. And since I'm not going to carry out the latter part of your plan, you don't need to either. You don't need to pay for my education courses. You've already given me too much."

"Lynne, what's this nonsense about money? I want you taking care of Tonio at Longridge. You promised you would and—"

"Did I?" she interrupted. "I don't remember that I did. I agreed to this—this charade—but I think then you suggested the rest and just assumed that like everyone else, I'd jump to obey."

He drew back, his mouth set in an uncompromising line. "I think that was uncalled for. I don't think I'm so harsh a master as you imply," he said stiffly, and she wept inside because she knew he was right. But she felt goaded, pushed beyond her endurance. She couldn't let him force her to go to Longridge, no matter what she had to say or do to get out of it.

"Furthermore," he went on, "you'll do as I say or you'll be very, very sorry."

"Threats?" she asked softly. "Well, I'm sure everyone who crosses swords with you is very, very sorry, but that doesn't change my mind."

She saw the dark glint of anger in his eyes, and

then suddenly his face softened. "Lynne, Lynne, what are we doing to each other? We're both worn out emotionally after yesterday, and who says travel and sightseeing aren't exhausting, too? Let's go back to the hotel. We'll shelve this discussion for now. You take a nap and we'll go out to dinner with Darren tonight—"

"I suppose you think a nice little nap and some good nourishing food will restore my deranged mind, so I'll say yes to anything you propose," she flung at him.

"What I was going to say was that we're both tired and saying things we don't mean. Let's not argue the point now. There's no need to make any decisions until after Tonio is legally mine."

"Perhaps not," she said, "but I don't think you are thinking of Tonio's welfare at this point. He's already lost both parents. You plan to take him from his grandparents for reasons you convinced me were good ones. But now you want him to spend the next six months becoming dependent on me. And then it will all change and I'll be taken away from him, too. He thinks of me as his aunt. It's hard enough on him to lose parents and grandparents without adding an aunt, too. You ought to give him a break—hire a nanny or governess, and either find one who will stay on, or at least let him know she's only temporary help. Or were you going to explain to him that I'm only his aunt for a season or two?"

He reached a hand toward her as if to speak, but then the moment passed, and his hand dropped to his lap. "This isn't the time for a serious discussion," he said. "You're overwrought, and no wonder. We'll talk tomorrow."

The dining room was elegant with a beautiful view. Soft yellow-gold silk lined the walls. Small bouquets of fresh flowers adorned each table, and a huge massed floral display formed a focus of interest on a large table in the center of the room.

Lynne had chosen the seat facing the window and watched as the lights of Florence began to come on in the deepening twilight.

When they had had their apéritif and ordered dinner, Darren told them about his day. The legal suit for custody of Tonio had been filed. He had also talked to Officer Siempe, who had checked with the wife of the leather shop owner and found that her story tallied exactly with Lynne's.

"I'll certainly have to buy some of her husband's leather goods," Jason said.

Darren shuddered. "When the case is won, you can buy the shop out if you like, but please, old boy, don't go near the place till then. It's true the police already have her statement, but we don't want anything that might even suggest the hint of a bribe."

Jason chuckled. "Talk about caution! But I'll take your advice."

"You'd better. You're paying me enough for it." He looked around with a satisfied air. "You know, we're fortunate that Tonio's grandparents are Florentine. Supposing we'd had to wait this out in some little Moldavian fishing village."

"Darren, you're crazy," Lynne said. "Anyway, there are probably some very picturesque Moldavian fishing villages."

"That doesn't seem likely," Jason said. "Moldavia isn't on the sea."

"Well, then, a goat-cheese processing village," Darren substituted. "I'm sure they must make goat-cheese."

"Of course," Lynne giggled. "Moldavian goat-cheese is famous all over the world."

She was feeling immeasurably better, listening to Darren's nonsense and forgetting about her personal problems.

The food was perfection. She was finishing the delicate veal dish she had ordered and admiring the view from the window, now that the sky was totally dark except for a handsome crescent moon, when suddenly she heard a voice behind her, a voice she would never forget, and all her pleasure in the food, the conversation, and the setting was ruined beyond repair.

"Well, isn't this cozy? A honeymoon for three. Do you suppose the idea will ever catch on?"

It was Justine Grant.

Lynne's eyes went to Jason and she was sure he was astonished to see her. Or was he? Could she be sure? Perhaps it was expecting too much that he could go for so long without the sight of her. Maybe this had been planned between them.

She glanced at Darren and was positive that his surprise was genuine. In fact, it was more like consternation. He was the first to speak, as both men rose to their feet.

"Justine, what the devil are you doing here?"

"What an ungracious greeting. Aren't you going to ask me to sit down?"

Lynne looked at her then for the first time. She was as beautiful as ever, her hair as silky, her eyes as green. Tonight she wore a dress that matched her eyes and was cut daringly low.

Jason seemed to be speechless. Darren said, "Aren't you with anyone? I don't think this is a good idea, Justine."

"Of course. I'm with friends, but they'll forgive me for slipping away for a bit. Now, are you going to help me to a chair or shall I do it myself?"

Reluctantly he held the chair for her. She turned to Jason. "My poor angel, you're looking so tired. Perhaps foreign travel doesn't agree with you." She turned toward Lynne then. "And the nanny-turned-bride. I can see you've done well by yourself on the trip." Her eyes had taken in the creamy ivory dinner dress Jason had bought for Lynne in Paris, and Lynne was sure she had been able to assess its value.

She was saved from having to speak by Darren's demanding, "You still haven't told us what you're doing in Florence."

"Oh, London was just unutterably dull so when some friends suggested a continental jaunt, I couldn't resist joining them. And now what a surprise to meet up with you. Such a small world!"

"Come off it, Justine," Darren said. "You knew perfectly well that we were in Florence. This is no accidental meeting. And I must say I don't like the idea."

Justine pouted prettily and turned to Jason. "I trust you aren't going to be as boorish as Darren. You'll always be glad to see an old friend, won't you?"

Darren cut in, "Don't be coy, Justine. This has nothing to do with whether any of us are glad to see you or not. The fact that you're here might jeopardize what we're all working for. Things are going well, but we have to be very careful. I don't want one hint of scandal. The farther you stay away from Jason, the better."

"But he has his little bride to chaperon him, surely. And his faithful watchdog."

"Justine, I think it would be better if you rejoined your friends." Jason's words were quiet but with a hint of steel.

Their eyes met and held, then she pushed back her chair. "Well, you will at least call me tomorrow,

won't you, pet? Here's my hotel and room number."
She put a slip of paper in his hand, rose gracefully,
blew a kiss, and was gone.

"Damn the woman," Darren said. "I'm sorry,
Jason, but she's not using good sense, coming here
like this. You're going to have to get rid of her."

"That should be easy. I have it on good authority
that everyone jumps to obey me," he said grimly.

The pleasant ambiance of the evening was irretriev-
ably gone. If Lynne swallowed anything more, she
couldn't taste it, didn't remember it. They made their
departure as quickly as they could. Even Darren's high
spirits had turned flat.

Lynne woke the next morning with a feeling of dull
misery. She couldn't face breakfast with Jason this
morning, not even if Darren were there to serve as a
buffer. She called down and had a tray sent to her
room.

When Jason phoned later, she told him she'd already eaten.

Darren had made an appointment for her to appear
with Jason in the judge's chambers for a brief interview.

It was an immense relief when it was over.

"You did beautifully," Darren said as they left the
building, giving her arm an encouraging squeeze.
"Very sincere. No one could help sensing your devotion and concern for the child. Considering your
appearance, Jason's position, and the irresponsible
dirty trickery the D'Allasios pulled in abducting
Tonio and lying to the police, I don't think we're
going to have any trouble at all."

If the judge had wondered why Mrs. Corey never
once looked at her husband during the interview,
perhaps he attributed it to nervousness, she thought.

"There are a few more papers you need to sign,

Jason," Darren said. "Would you like to come along, Lynne?"

She shook her head. "I believe I'll go for a walk and do some more sightseeing. I'll probably just have a bite somewhere along the way, so you two go ahead and have lunch."

She escaped from them with a feeling of relief. The air was crisp and the walk helped a little. She had no planned itinerary; her path was an aimless one, and yet everywhere in Florence there was something interesting to see, some balm to the spirit.

After several hours, feeling somewhat better, she started back across the Ponte Vecchio toward the hotel when suddenly the sight of a figure she could mistake for no other stopped her in her tracks. No one had quite his look of elegant strength. No one carried himself with quite his decisive, purposeful movement. It was Jason and he was coming out of one of the jewelry shops along the bridge. She couldn't tell from this distance which of the lovely shops it was, but he was carrying a package.

Justine hadn't been in town twenty-four hours and already he was buying her a present.

She felt heartsick anew. She walked on, determining that if she saw him returning to the hotel, she would continue walking. She didn't want any sort of confrontation with him now.

When she was across the bridge, she saw that he had turned left and was walking away from the hotel —probably to see Justine, she thought, in spite of Darren's warning. Well, since when was love wise?

Knowing that she could safely count on being alone, she went into the hotel and up to her room. She decided to wash out some hose in the basin, grateful for an ordinary task to keep her busy.

It was well past lunchtime, but she hadn't eaten

yet. She decided she'd just have a sandwich on a tray in her room. When she had finished, she put the tray on the floor in the hallway and hung a Do Not Disturb sign on her door. The long walk in the fresh air had made her sleepy, and goodness knows she hadn't slept much the night before. She lay down to take a nap and fell asleep almost at once.

She was in such a deep slumber that when the knocking woke her, she didn't know where she was. She groped her way to full consciousness, opened a curtain, and looked at her watch. It was late afternoon. The knocking at the door continued, imperiously.

She slipped into a robe—not the pretty one Madelaine had given her, but the conservative brown one—and opened the door.

Justine Grant stood there tapping her foot impatiently. "It took you long enough to answer," she said ungraciously.

"What do you want?"

"I stopped by the hotel to see Jason, but he wasn't in his room."

"I don't know where he is." Her answer was short, and she tried to close the door, but Justine pushed it open and came in uninvited.

"My, my, such a short time married and already losing track of the bridegroom," she purred wickedly, choosing an armchair and sitting down. "Doesn't he ever report in before he takes off?"

"I was taking a nap and had a Do Not Disturb sign on the door. Jason wouldn't be rude enough to disregard it," she said pointedly, and opened the other curtains to let more light into the room.

"So the kitten has claws after all," Justine said, crossing one slim leg over the other and swinging her ankle. "You really ought to treat me a little nicer. It

143

would be so easy for me to ruin your little scheme."

Lynne looked at her in surprise. "I don't know what you mean."

"Suppose I told the D'Allasios your marriage was nothing but a hoax—a cheap trick so that Jason could get custody of Tonio. If their lawyers were armed with that information, you wouldn't stand a chance."

"I wouldn't stand a chance!" Lynne repeated in amazement. "It's Jason who's fighting for custody. Anyway, you wouldn't do that."

"And why not?" Justine's tone was insolent.

"Because Jason would never forgive you."

Justine's lips curved in a slow, knowing smile. "There's very little a man won't eventually forgive a woman he loves if she knows how to earn forgiveness."

This woman made her flesh crawl. "There's another reason you won't do it," Lynne said. "Why should they believe you? I'm his wife—you're the discarded ex-fiancée, the woman scorned, spreading lies out of spite. You'd make a laughing-stock of yourself."

Justine's eyelids narrowed in fury, but Lynne had had enough of her. "Now get out of my room. I'm going to dress for dinner. And if you don't want it spread around that you went chasing across Europe after a man while he was on his honeymoon, then stay away from the D'Allasios. Remember—I'm the one with the license, the ring, and his name. There's no reason why anyone would believe you."

When she had closed and locked the door, she leaned against it, shaking.

The telephone shrilled, startling her. She didn't want to answer it. Surely it couldn't be Justine phoning from the lobby, but she didn't want to talk to

Jason either. It kept on ringing and finally she picked up the receiver.

A crisp, cool voice said, "Madelaine Cheney here. I've been calling Mr. Corey but he doesn't answer, so I thought I'd try you."

"Oh, Madelaine," Lynne cried, glad to hear a friendly voice. Then realizing that this was a business call, she said, "He isn't in the hotel right now. Shall I have him call you back later?"

"Yes, if you please. How are you getting on?"

That was a poser. Finally she said, "Darren Lloyd showed up the day before yesterday, you know. He seems to think the legal matter is looking quite hopeful."

"I see. And you. How are you getting on?"

"Why, I—Florence is very beautiful," she stammered.

"Then what's wrong? And don't say 'nothing,' because your voice gives you away."

"Oh, Madelaine, Justine arrived last night," Lynne said in a tone of despair. "Darren is furious because he says her hanging around Jason may jeopardize the case. He's told Jason to get rid of her, but I don't know if he'll be able to if she digs her heels in. I don't even know if he wants to. And Madelaine, I know this is foolish, but she frightens me. I can't explain it. She came here looking for Jason this afternoon and—well, I wonder if she's quite sane. Maybe I'm just dramatizing, but lately I've realized what lengths some people will go to to get their own way. And I think she's one of those people."

"Mmm. Suppose I had some papers that Mr. Corey needed to sign personally. Suppose I just flew over to Florence. Do you think an extra friendly shoulder to lean on might be of any help?"

"Oh, if you only could," Lynne breathed. "I'd be so glad of a friend."

"I'll manage to find some urgent problem which needs Jason's immediate attention."

"I don't want you to get in trouble on my account."

Madelaine gave a low laugh. "Never fear. I didn't get to be an executive secretary without learning how to assume responsibility. Now, don't worry. Just guard the fort meanwhile."

Guard the fort, Lynne thought wearily, hanging up the phone. That was easy enough to say, but there was danger of different kinds from many directions to guard against. Who was to say which was the most dangerous of all—Justine, the D'Allasios, Jason, or her own unruly heart?

CHAPTER TWELVE

Lynne, Darren, and Jason ate dinner in a small *trattoria*. As if by mutual consent, Justine's name was not mentioned. If Darren had questioned Jason as to whether he had tried to persuade her to leave Florence, he had apparently done it earlier, as the subject did not come up during dinner.

Lynne did not mention her own unpleasant interview with Justine either. She could not tell Jason that Justine had threatened to ruin their hopes of getting custody of Tonio. He would never believe such a thing of the woman he loved, and Lynne wouldn't blame him for that. It was so incredible she could hardly believe it herself.

Jason seemed distinctly cool and remote, but whether he was still annoyed over their disagreement of yesterday or whether he was thinking of Justine, Lynne didn't know.

Even Darren seemed somewhat abstracted, though he politely asked Lynne how she had spent her day.

"I took a long walk this morning and a nap this afternoon."

"I'm going to need you with me tomorrow, Jason," Darren said.

He nodded, then said to Lynne, "By the way, Miss Cheney is flying in tomorrow. I have some work that needs to be taken care of. She'll probably be here several days."

"I'll be happy to see her," Lynne said, her sense of depression lightening at the welcome news.

* * *

Madelaine's plane arrived shortly after noon, so Lynne waited to have lunch with her. She left a message at the desk to have her call as soon as she checked in.

She was waiting in her room for the phone, but a knock came at the door instead. She almost dreaded opening it in fear it might be Justine again. When she saw Madelaine there instead, her face lit up and she clasped both of the older woman's hands in hers and pulled her into the room.

"Now then," Madelaine said in her no-nonsense tone, "why were you looking like grim death when you opened the door? And what have you been doing to yourself? Your clothes are terrific, but your eyes do not have the look of a happy tourist."

"You must be starved," Lynne said. "Let's have lunch and talk then. You're all checked in? Is your room satisfactory?"

Madelaine nodded and Lynne snatched up her purse and they went out.

"Explain those dark shadows," Madelaine demanded after they had ordered.

"The last few days have been a strain," she said and recounted the story of Tonio's abduction. "And then, just as we seemed out of the woods, Justine showed up. As I told you on the phone, Darren thinks it's dangerous to have her here."

"And what about Mr. Corey?"

Lynne spread her hands helplessly. "I don't know. I haven't discussed it with him."

"I should have thought that by this—" Madelaine started and then checked herself in midsentence. "Tell me why you think she's deranged."

"I know this sounds unbelievable but I swear it's

148

true. She said I should treat her better because she could easily ruin our little scheme—those were her words—by telling the D'Allasios our marriage was a hoax."

"Well, that's laying it right on the line. What did you say?"

"I told her Jason would never forgive her. She seemed to think there were ways of making a man forgive anything." Lynne grimaced with distaste. "So then I pointed out that I would merely deny it to the D'Allasios and their legal counsel, and it would be dismissed as a spiteful story told by Jason's ex-girl-friend, whom he had left for me."

"So now she won't try that," Madelaine said slow-ly. "At least not directly. But if she could show them it was true . . ."

"But that's just crazy!" Lynne cried. "It's Jason she'd really be hurting, not me. Whatever happens, I won't be involved with Tonio for much longer. I don't see why she'd even think of doing such a thing."

"I wonder," Madelaine said slowly. "Do you sup-pose he told her about his plan to have you go back to Longridge and look after Tonio for a while?"

"I don't know. But anyway—"

"Because if he did . . ." Madelaine seemed to be thinking aloud. "If he did, it would make sense all right. Don't you see, if she eliminates Tonio from Jason's life, she gets rid of you at the same stroke."

"Gets rid of me?" Lynne echoed in surprise.

"Gets you out of Jason's life. If he loses the custody battle, there'd be no reason to continue with the marriage, no reason for you to go to Longridge. You'd be paid off and on your way. That's the way she'd look at it."

"But I'll be out of his life very shortly anyway," Lynne said, her voice not quite steady. "I'm only an employee. She knows that."

"What a sweet innocent you are," Madelaine said dryly. "Look, I imagine it was galling to her to have Jason go through the marriage ceremony with you to begin with. I'm sure she never agreed to it willingly. But when Jason Corey makes up his mind—"

"I know," Lynne said. "He's an autocrat."

"A determined man is the way I'd put it," Madelaine said. "Anyway, it's obvious she came to Florence to look the situation over, and size up just how risky it was to her. She might have been expecting lovesick letters and phone calls from Mr. Corey all along the way and wasn't getting them. So she came here to see how matters stood, and apparently she didn't like what she saw."

Lynne was incredulous. "You can't mean that she was jealous! There's no reason for her to think—"

"Maybe, maybe not. If he'd been calling her or writing to her every day to say how much he missed her, very likely she wouldn't have worried. So we can pretty well assume that he wasn't calling or writing. Therefore it must have seemed logical to her to come here and see for herself just how involved he was with you."

"There was nothing to see."

"Mmm," Madelaine said. "Describe this first meeting with her."

"We were having dinner at a very elegant restaurant, but that was because we were supposed to be celebrating the fact that Tonio's kidnapping had turned out all right."

"And you were wearing a Paris gown," Madelaine put in.

"Well, yes, but it wasn't a *tête-à-tête*. Darren was with us."

"And Darren was furious, you said. How did Mr. Corey react?"

"He seemed surprised. I wasn't sure if he really was or if it was just an act. After a while, when Darren kept telling her she mustn't hang about, Jason said she'd better rejoin her friends. Then Darren said Jason would have to get her to leave Florence. I don't know whether he tried or not, but she didn't leave. I think he bought her a present the next day, and I assumed he went to see her. Then in the afternoon she came to the hotel looking for him and, when she couldn't find him, she knocked on my door instead."

"In a foul mood," Madelaine said. "So if Jason had seen her earlier in the day, the interview must not have reassured her."

"Reassured her about what? There's no way she could imagine I could provide any competition for her!"

"No, you were just sitting there in an elegant restaurant, wearing a beautiful gown Jason had bought you, being wined and dined, and when she showed up he certainly didn't fall on her neck with glad cries. In her place, I think I'd be jealous, too. Have you told him about what Justine said when she came to see you?"

Lynne drew back. "Certainly not. How could I go to him bearing tales about Justine? Anyway, I don't suppose he'd even believe me."

"Why? Does he have some reason to doubt your word?"

Lynne looked uncomfortable. "Well, perhaps he thinks so. You see, he's been assuming that I would go back to Longridge and care for Tonio for six

151

months or so, since Justine isn't free to marry him yet anyway, but two days ago I told him I wasn't prepared to do that."

Madelaine sighed. "Back to square one. You were behaving like an idiot the first time I met you, and you're at it again. Why don't you want to go to Longridge?"

"It would be hard on Tonio," Lynne said a little too promptly. "I'm supposedly his aunt now. If he gets used to living with me and then I disappear—just like his parents disappeared—how is that going to affect him?"

"And that's the only reason?" Madelaine's eyes were penetrating.

Lynne looked away. "I don't want to get too attached to Tonio either. It will be hard giving him up now. Think what it would be like six months from now."

"And I suppose it hasn't occurred to you that in six months— No, I'm sure it hasn't." She sat back. "Well, let's take it one step at a time. I agree that Justine is dangerous. We're going to have to be on our guard. Meanwhile, don't say anymore to Mr. Corey about not going to Longridge. He has enough on his mind. Just sit tight for the present. Agreed?"

"Agreed," Lynne said, but she felt unhappy about it. While it was a comfort to have Madelaine Cheney there, Lynne felt she should be on her guard against her, too. She had the uneasy feeling that Madelaine saw too much.

The weather was still fine and next morning the four of them breakfasted together on the roof— Lynne, Jason, Madelaine, and Darren. The same four, Lynne reflected, who had composed the wedding party luncheon a few days, but a lifetime, ago.

"Darren needs me to sign some legal papers this morning," Jason said. "Maddy, if you'll have those contracts from the office ready, we'll plan to begin work about two o'clock."

"Very well, sir," Madelaine said.

A waiter approached the table. "There is a phone call for Signora Corey. If you will come with me, please."

"For me?" Lynne was puzzled. "Are you sure it isn't for Signor Corey?"

"No, Signora. For you."

Uncertainly she rose and followed him. Whom did she know that might be calling her here?

When she returned a few minutes later, she was wearing a somewhat bewildered expression. "That was Isabella D'Allasio," she announced. "She said she regretted the misunderstandings between us and that she felt we should get to know each other better. She invited me to lunch. Do you think it's all right for me to go?"

"Things couldn't be much worse between us than they are already," Jason said. "I don't see how it could hurt. What do you think, Darren?"

"I suppose it's all right," he said, frowning. "Still, it seems most uncharacteristic."

Madelaine calmly spread butter on her roll, but there was a look of watchful alertness in her eyes.

When they had finished eating, Madelaine went with Lynne to her room. "Since you're going to be out anyway, would you mind giving me a key to your room?" she asked. "I suppose Mr. Corey and I will work in the sitting room next door. I may want to freshen up and this would be more convenient than going down to my floor."

Lynne handed her the key. "I can get the other one from the desk. If preparing the contracts won't take all morning, perhaps you'd like to do a bit of sight-seeing. The Piazza del Duomo isn't far, nor the Uffizi."

"Splendid. I have an errand to take care of, but I could be ready in fifteen minutes."

"I'll meet you in the lobby, then," Lynne said.

At eleven thirty Madelaine said, "I believe I'd better go back to the hotel and start work on those contracts."

"Yes, and I'll get ready for my luncheon date. Why do I feel so nervous?"

In the restaurant Isabella D'Allasio had specified Lynne was shown to a corner table. Again dressed in black, Isabella sat, with her back erect, smoking a cigarette. The remains of three cigarettes were already in the ashtray, though Lynne was not late for the appointment. Perhaps the Signora was nervous, too.

She motioned for a waiter, who filled Lynne's wine glass. Lynne waited for her to begin, but there were no words, only the piercing gaze of the obsidian eyes.

Lynne moistened her lips. "Signora D'Allasio, you said you wanted to talk."

"What can one say? You wish to take my grandson from me."

"Signora, had Tonio's father lived, he would soon have gone back to England, and entered Tonio in an English school. My husband is carrying out his brother's wishes."

"His brother is dead. Are his wishes more important than those of the living?"

She drained her glass and refilled it from the bottle the waiter had left on the table. Lynne wondered if she had been drinking for a long time. There was something unusually odd about her manner.

"It is not only the wish of his brother," Lynne said.

"It is the wish of my husband also to raise Tonio as his own son. You have raised a daughter to womanhood. Can't you be content to remain Tonio's grandparents? Surely your interest must lie in another direction than child-rearing. It is a time of life when you should be free to travel, not to be worrying about whether a small child has a sore throat or is having nightmares. And you will always be his grandparents, welcome to visit him at any time, to spend a week or a month at Longridge whenever you wish."

"You think we wish him to be raised by a man like that?" She spat the words out.

Lynne drew back. "I don't know what you mean," she said stiffly. "A man like what? My husband is a respected businessman. He's—"

The Signora leaned forward, a malicious gleam playing in her eyes. "And is he a faithful husband—even on your honeymoon?"

"I'm sorry," Lynne said coldly, "but I don't believe I shall stay for lunch. It seems we have nothing to talk about after all."

She rose but the Signora's hand snaked out and caught her wrist. "No, it is too early. You can't go back yet."

"Too early for what, Signora?" Her eyes widened. She and Madelaine had agreed they must be on guard against Justine, but she hadn't heeded the suspicious fact that Signora D'Allasio had invited her to lunch—a most unexpected act. Had it been to lure her away from the hotel, making sure that Jason would be alone?

She pulled away from the clawlike hand and rushed from the restaurant.

She was short of breath from hurrying when she reached the hotel. As she got out of the lift on her floor, she saw two men knocking at Jason's bedroom door. The door of the sitting room between the two bedrooms opened instead.

Jason was standing in the doorway with a look of impersonal inquiry on his face, but behind him, across the room, Lynne saw an astonishing scene. Justine was lying on a settee with her blouse undone. Over her stood the redoubtable Miss Cheney, every hair in place, dashing the water from a vase of flowers in Justine's face.

Justine sat up spluttering and Madelaine said calmly, "I think she's coming around, sir."

Jason spun around and the two strangers pushed into the room, with Lynne following.

"I am Guido Faretti, legal advisor for the D'Allasio family, and this is a witness from the court," the taller of the two men announced.

"What we need is a doctor," Madelaine said and then clutching at Justine's wrist, she added, "No, I believe her pulse is growing stronger."

"Can you explain the meaning of this, sir?" Faretti asked belligerently.

"Why the devil should I explain anything to you?" Jason demanded angrily.

"It's quite simple," Madeline said coolly to Signor Faretti. "I was taking dictation from Mr. Corey when Mrs. Grant arrived looking for Mrs. Corey. She said she was leaving town and wanted to say good-bye. Mr. Corey told her his wife had been invited to have lunch with Signora D'Allasio. Mrs. Grant said she'd like to wait. She went over and sat down and we continued with our work.

"Suddenly she said she was feeling faint and seemed to go into a swoon. I loosened her clothing and chafed her wrists but to no avail, so Mr. Corey suggested water. As you can see, it seems to have brought her around."

"Perhaps you'd like to come into my room now," Lynne said to the enraged Justine. "We must get you out of that wet blouse. I can loan you one of mine."

Madelaine took one of her arms, not too gently, and Lynne the other, and they led her from the room as Guido Faretti was saying to Jason, "My apologies, Signore. We seem to have made a mistake."

When Jason had closed the door behind them, he came to Lynne's room. "Now, what is this all about?" He was staring sternly at Madelaine. "How did you happen to appear just as those men came to the door?"

"Mrs. Corey gave me the key to her room in case I needed to freshen up during the afternoon while we worked. I had finished lunch and remembered she'd recommended a guide book which was on her dresser. Since I had some spare time, I thought I'd come and have a look at it. While I was reading it I heard a loud knocking. I didn't realize you were in the sitting room, but it sounded as if the knocking were on that door, so I went through the connecting door from the bedroom into the sitting room to answer it. When I saw Mrs. Grant lying on the settee, I revived her with the water in the flower vase." She paused as if struck by a sudden thought. "I must refill it and put the flowers back before they wilt."

"That can wait. I don't believe you've finished your explanation," Jason said dryly.

"When the man at the door said he was the D'Allasios legal counsel, it occurred to me that it would be best if he thought Mrs. Grant had come to see Mrs. Corey and that I had been in the room the whole time, which is why I said what I did. That's all. I'll attend to the flowers now."

She went into the other room, leaving a tense group of three behind her. "If Mrs. Grant is quite recovered," Lynne said smoothly, "I'll take her back to her hotel so you and Miss Cheney can get on with your work, Jason."

She could have sworn Jason flashed her a grateful look as he went out.

"Would you like to borrow a dry blouse?" she asked Justine sweetly.

"A blouse of yours? Not likely!" Justine was furious. "This one was pure silk and it's ruined."

"What a shame. Are you feeling well enough to leave now?"

Justine didn't deign to speak again but as she stalked out, she flashed Lynne a look of pure venom.

Lynne could hardly wait to talk privately with Madelaine, but as she knew Jason would keep her working for the afternoon, she decided to visit a museum to calm down her seething emotions.

At five o'clock she was back in her room and before long Madelaine knocked. Lynne pulled her inside. "I've been dying to talk to you. I've heard your explanation to the two witnesses, and then your explanation to Jason. Now I want the real version."

Madelaine sat down and lit a cigarette. "I'm afraid it will have to be mostly conjecture. From what I had heard of the D'Allasios it seemed peculiar for the Signora to have invited you to lunch. If there was some reason for wanting you out of the way, I thought it might be a good idea to keep an eye on what was happening here. That's why I asked for the key to your room.

"Now here's where the conjecture comes in. I can

only suppose that Justine must have called Mr. Corey and made some excuse for needing to see him."

"That shouldn't have been too difficult," Lynne said.

"No," Madelaine agreed. "She might have told him she was leaving town and had to talk to him before she left. That would sound logical and would be hard for him to refuse. Meanwhile, the D'Allasios must have been told that if they could get you out of the way and get a witness here, they could get evidence that Mr. Corey was morally unfit to be appointed Tonio's guardian."

"Do you suppose she contacted them directly?"

"Somehow I doubt she'd tip her hand that way. I think it more likely that she sent an anonymous note saying that if his wife were out of the way this afternoon, Mr. Corey would be having as assignation with another woman."

"It was lucky they were in the sitting room rather than the bedroom."

"Not exactly luck," Madelaine said. "I took the precaution of calling the housekeeper this morning and telling her that Mr. Corey didn't want his room made up till after lunch. While I was waiting in here, I could hear Mr. Corey and Justine talking in the sitting room. I had your door to the corridor open a crack so I heard the knocking. I picked up my papers and went through the connecting door to the sitting room immediately. As Mr. Corey went to the door, I saw Justine lie back on the settee and undo the top buttons of her blouse. So I just picked up the vase and poured water on her."

"You're a wonder," Lynne said admiringly. "Do you suppose Jason realizes it was a trap? How on earth can Justine ever explain to him why she lay down on the couch as soon as she heard knocking. I should have thought she'd be afraid it would ruin her with Jason forever, pulling such a stunt."

"You underestimate her," Madelaine said. "She's totally ruthless. She'll think of something. For instance, she might say that you had talked to her and tried to warn her off—told her that Jason had fallen out of love with her and into love with you. And when she heard someone at the door, she thought it was you and just wanted to teach you a lesson. It's not a pretty story, but it's prettier than the real one. I can just hear her." She mimicked Justine's way of talking. "Oh, Jason, I'm so sorry I was thoughtless, but of course I had no idea you were being spied upon by those dreadful people, or I never would have come. I thought it was that awful girl at the door and she'd been so insulting to me, telling me you didn't care about me anymore. I just had this sudden impulse to show the catty little creature that I wasn't so easily fooled. That's why I lay down on the settee."

Lynne was frowning in perplexity. "I can understand her resenting me and wanting to get rid of me. But if she really tried to ruin Jason's chances of getting custody of Tonio . . ." Her voice trailed off. "You said she was totally ruthless. If that's so, am I doing the right thing in helping Jason in this matter? Is it morally right to help put Tonio in a position where a year from now Justine Grant will have a position of authority in his life?"

There was the merest hint of a smile on Madelaine's lips. After a moment she said, "I wouldn't worry about that if I were you."

"I can't help worrying. I don't like his grandparents, but I'm not sure I want to be responsible for turning him over to Justine either. And maybe I'm being unfair to the D'Allasios. They tried to trick us, it's true, but after all, Jason and I have been dishonest with them, too, pretending to a marriage that doesn't exist—except on paper."

"However, you and Jason haven't used the child as a helpless pawn the way his grandparents did, frightening and upsetting him into hysterics by having him abducted."

"That's true," Lynne said, but she still looked unhappy.

"See here, my little idiot, didn't you promise me you'd quit fretting about the future and just take things one step at a time? Put Justine out of your mind. It's quite possible that a happier solution for Tonio will be found in time."

Lynne didn't know what she meant, but Madelaine gave one of her enigmatic smiles and said no more.

CHAPTER THIRTEEN

The next morning Jason and Darren had business to attend to, and Madelaine had some calls to the office in London to make and papers to put in order. Lynne decided she would go to the Pitti Palace and visit the art gallery. When her mind was troubled, it helped to concentrate on the visual impressions of a bygone age.

She was nearly there when she heard a hateful voice behind her saying, "Stop a minute, Mrs. Corey. I want to talk to you."

She turned with a sigh. How could she forget her troubles if they persisted in tracking her down?

"I've been following you," Justine said. "I want to talk to you."

There seemed no way to avoid her. "All right, let's go into the Gardens and sit down," Lynne said resignedly.

"I suppose you and that secretary think you're pretty smart. But it won't do you any good. No matter what tale you told Jason about me, I can think up a better one. And I know how to make him believe mine."

"I'm sure you do," Lynne said steadily, "but as it happens we didn't tell him any tale about you at all. He's free to draw his own conclusions."

"Why don't you give it up and go home? You'll never get what you want out of this."

"Believe me, I'd like nothing better than to go home. The only thing I want out of this is what's best for Tonio—though I'm not sure I know what that is anymore. You seem determined to misinterpret the situation, but everything Jason and I have done has been intended for Tonio's good."

"Tonio's good!" Justine sneered. "Your pure and noble act really nauseates me. Tonio's good! You know as well as I do that money is what the battle is all about."

Guilt stabbed at Lynne as she thought of the money Jason had paid to cancel her debt to Uncle Simon. She realized that Justine would have been told that she was hired to marry Jason, but had he discussed the price, the reason she needed the money? Somehow she felt betrayed. "It was not such a large amount," she said stiffly. "It won't diminish the estate so much that you'll be impoverished."

"What?" Justine said harshly. "You don't think I'm talking about any paltry sum he may have paid for your services, do you?"

Lynne looked puzzled.

"I'm talking about half the Corey Company. That's what this is all about. Jason's father left the business to him and Morgan in equal shares. Tonio inherited Morgan's half. Why else do you think Jason wants guardianship of a half-foreign brat who doesn't even speak English? With Tonio in his custody, he won't have to answer to anybody about the way he runs the business or where the profits go. Do you think he'd let a prize like that slip through his fingers so easily, when fate was kind enough to orphan his nephew? And of course if anything should happen to Tonio, who but his guardian uncle would get it all?"

Lynne felt sick. It couldn't be true. "I don't understand you," she whispered. "These accusations—they're against the man you love, the man you want to marry. Surely you don't mean what you're saying."

Justine gave a short, hard laugh. "Do you think it matters to me? My father was in big business. It's in my blood. I know how the game is played, and it doesn't bother me. In fact, that streak of ruthlessness in Jason makes him all the more desirable and exciting in my eyes. If a milk and water miss like you can't stomach it, then do your noble duty and get away from him."

"If I walk out on him now before the papers are signed, he may very well lose Tonio," she said slowly, almost more to herself than Justine.

"Which is fine with me," Justine said. "I have no desire to bring up another woman's child. I don't blame Jason for trying to get his hands on Tonio's inheritance, but if he fails—well, I'm not greedy. Half the company is plenty for me."

Lynne got up from the bench and backed away, eyeing Justine as one would a loathsome and dangerous serpent that one has come upon unawares. She turned and, stumbling, fled up the path.

It couldn't be true. If it were, how could she ever believe in anything again? She had let herself be used knowingly, but she had believed it was for a good reason. Had she only convinced herself it was for a good reason because she wanted the money she would be paid? No, that wasn't true. She really loved Tonio and wanted what was best for him. But if what Justine said was true and it was all a plot to get hold of Tonio's inheritance, then she was responsible for a terrible injustice.

A hand reached out and caught her arm just as she was about to enter the hotel. "Slow down a minute, Lynne. What's the matter? You look as if you've been seeing ghosts." It was Darren.

"I was just hurrying," she said. "Let me catch my

breath. There's something I want to ask you. Did Jason's father own the Corey Company before him?"

"Yes, of course, though Jason has expanded it a good deal." He was clearly puzzled by the question.

"And Jason inherited it?"

He nodded. "He and Morgan together."

"Then half of everything was Morgan's?"

"Half the stock. He chose not to work in the business. Jason had the director's salary in addition, but half the holdings were Morgan's."

"And now Tonio has inherited it?"

"Certainly. What's this all about, Lynne?"

She shook her head, not trusting herself to speak.

Inside her room she flung herself across the bed. "Be on your guard against Justine," Madelaine had said. Well, clearly Justine was a viper, and Lynne wouldn't have taken her word for anything, but Darren had confirmed it. What Justine had said was true.

She wept until she had no more tears—for herself, for Tonio, perhaps most of all for her loss of innocence.

She had believed it—bought the whole story. Oh, they'd done a job on her, all right—Madelaine, Darren, Jason.

Jason. Well, she was cured of him now. Never again would her breath catch at the sight of him, her flesh tremble where his hand accidently brushed it, or her heart sing at the sound of his voice.

She could love in secret a man who wasn't hers; she could have built dreams on him to last a lonely lifetime. But she couldn't love a man she despised and knowing what she knew, she despised him now. Never never again would her blood burn for him.

It was over, and she felt empty.

Perhaps as a protective mechanism against any

further thought, any further facing of reality, she fell into a deep sleep.

She was awakened by Jason's voice and knock at the door. She stumbled from bed and looked at the clock in amazement. In her state of emotional exhaustion, she'd slept half the day away. Her clothes were rumpled, her hair in disarray, but she didn't care.

She opened the door, her heart hardened against the sight of him. He looked particularly exuberant, his gray eyes glowing. How easily he moves, she thought, as if all the muscles under his elegantly cut suits had the sinewy, flowing strength of a jungle cat. But he would never move her again; the way his dark hair lay on his neck would never arouse in her the desire to touch him, to run her hand across the back of his neck, her fingers moving under his hair.

"Come in; I have something to say to you." Her husky voice was flat and expressionless.

"And I have something to tell you—"

She interrupted him, intent on bringing it out into the open at once. "I can't go on with this, Jason. I want no part of it. I made a terrible mistake and I suppose I can never really rectify it, but I'll try. I'll pay back the money you sent my uncle. It will take awhile but—"

"Oh, do be quiet about the money, Lynne. What's this all about?"

"It's all about money, after all," she said sadly. "I thought it was about something quite different, but it was only money. That's the point."

"Are you so upset about my seeing Justine yesterday?"

"Of course not," she said wearily. "You can see whomever you please. Why not?"

"It was an ill-considered thing to do, but she called and insisted she had to see me before she left Florence. I felt I owed her that much."

How could a man who looked so honest and open be so deceitful, she wondered.

"That has nothing to do with it," Lynne said. "I was just mistaken, that's all. You three had such plausible reasons why Tonio must become your ward. I was convinced. Or maybe I convinced myself because I was greedy for the money, as greedy in my small way as you. But I did love Tonio, and your plausible reasons sounded so right. But my eyes are open now, and I'll have no part of it. I think I should warn you, Jason, I'm going to the D'Allasios' lawyer and tell him our marriage is a hoax. I'll do everything I need to in order to keep you from getting Tonio into your clutches."

He had been watching her first with amazement, then with distress, but now a surge of pure anger suffused his face, lighting a furious fire in his eyes.

"Oh, you will, will you?" His voice was low and harsh. "I think you've run mad. After all we've been through together, fighting for Tonio! And now you're going to keep him out of my clutches, are you? Well, if you think you can set yourself against me in this, you can think again."

"What are you going to do, Jason? Kill me to keep me from telling the truth? Put your hands around my throat and choke me into silence?"

He grabbed her shoulders in a steely grip. "By God, it's not a bad idea." He let her go as if he had suddenly come to his senses. "It's not necessary. Your conversion came too late. That's what I was coming to tell you. The final papers were signed this afternoon. Tonio is mine now."

The words pierced a tender place in her chest. She

had delivered Tonio into the hands of a monster. She loved the child, and she was his betrayer.

"I'll find a way to protect him from you, Jason. I swear I will."

"You are mad," he said wonderingly. "We'll gloss over the fact that you're disloyal, ungrateful, that you can't be trusted to keep a bargain. All this time I've been traveling with a mad woman, sharing experiences, laughing with her, thinking she was—discovering I—"

It was the first time she had ever heard Jason incoherent. Then he stopped the flow of seemingly random words and said quite precisely, "Crazy or not, you're coming with me to the villa to pick up Tonio. The D'Allasios know we're coming. They'll have his things ready."

She shook her head. "I won't be a part of it."

He grabbed her again and his fingers pressed into her shoulders hard enough to bruise. "You'll do as I say. You're standing in clothes I've bought, in a room I've paid for, and you dare to tell me you won't do the one thing you were hired for! You'll come if I have to drag you by your lovely hair, if I have to knock some sense into your lovely lying head."

His hand like a vise on her arm, he propelled her to the door as she resisted with all her strength. She was powerless before him.

Suddenly she relaxed. He would hardly dare to drag her through the lobby this way, would he?— though perhaps there was nothing he wouldn't dare. But she had realized she must go with him after all. Hating him, hating the situation, still she must accompany him. In the mood he was in she couldn't leave him alone with Tonio.

The child would be frightened seeing his uncle in this white-mouthed rage. He wouldn't be able to talk

to him. At least if she were there she could soothe
the child, hold him in her arms on the drive back
to the hotel, try to protect him. She made no further
resistance.

As the powerful car purred through the night, a
sense of total desolation swept her. It was not that she
had lost Jason. How could you lose what you had
never had? But she had lost her love for him, her
foolish, hopeless love. She should be glad to lose
something that could only bring her pain. Then why
did it hurt so much? Why did she feel more alone
as she sat here beside him than she had ever felt in
her life?

They pulled up to the villa, which was dark except for the lower part in the right wing where the
living and drawing rooms were. Several cars stood in
the drive. The front door was partly open.

Jason rang. She could hear the bell echoing through
the house. No one came. He rang again, imperiously.
They waited, but still no one came.

"What sort of game are they playing?" he muttered.
"Come on. We're going in."

He pushed open the door and pulled her inside.
"D'Allasio!" he shouted.

There was only silence.

He crossed the hall to the drawing room, Lynne
behind him. As the door swung back, light spilled
out into the hallway.

Peering around Jason, Lynne was met with a most
peculiar sight. The D'Allasios and Vincente were
there. She also recognized Paola Malina, and there
were several others. They were all sitting in odd
attitudes of relaxation, one man on the floor leaning against a wall, Paola lying back on a couch with
her shoes off.

"D'Allasio, what's the meaning of this?" Jason

barked. "No one answered the door. You don't think you can stop us from—"

Suddenly he stopped and gave a snort of disgust.

Lynne felt as if she were viewing some strange nightmare sequence. They moved, not in alarm or surprise, but in what almost seemed slow motion. Their expressions were vapid, their eyes black and expressionless. She began to shiver.

"What's wrong with them?" she whispered.

"Drugged," he said. "It's a drug party. And isn't that a pretty sight to treat a child to? Opium, I shouldn't wonder."

"Matteo, where's Tonio?" He shook the older man by the shoulder roughly, but received only a foolish smile.

"Jason, what's that strange odor. Is it the opium?"

He looked up, his senses alert. Then he moved quickly. "No, by God, it's smoke—not opium smoke, a fire!"

She dashed after him as he ran from the room. Which way was Tonio's room?

"Call the fire department," he flung at her over his shoulder and went bounding up the steps two at a time.

With shaking hands she made the call and went back to the drawing room. "The house is on fire," she shouted. "You must tell me where Tonio is!"

"It doesn't matter," Isabella said very slowly. "He doesn't live here now. Francesca doesn't live here now. Hardly anyone lives here now."

"Tell me where he is!" Lynne's frantic hands shook the woman by the shoulders, but she only closed her eyes.

"If you can't help, then all of you get out of here. Don't you understand? The house is burning!"

"Nero burned while Rome fiddled," Paola giggled.

They were hopeless. Perhaps she could lead them out one by one if they were too stupified to understand, but not until after Tonio was safe.

She raced upstairs and almost collided with Jason, who was running back from searching the upper rooms of the right wing. "He's not there or here in the central portion. He must be in the left wing, and that's where the fire is."

"Could the servants have taken him somewhere? None of them seem to be around."

"We can't take a chance on it," he said grimly.

They ran into the left wing and began to choke on the smoke which filled the corridor. They rounded a corner and could see flames licking out of one of the rooms, making their way across the carpet and along the wall.

Jason was shouting Tonio's name, and at last they heard a small cry. He was standing at the far end of the corridor beyond the area that was ablaze but the fire was moving toward him and blocking the path to the spot where he stood.

"Get me some wet towels," Jason ordered. "Stand still, Tonio, I'm coming."

Lynne realized the boy couldn't understand Jason's words and shouted to him in Italian as she ran into a bathroom and soaked several towels.

Jason wrapped one around the lower part of his face to breath through and poised for a second, preparing to dash through the flames.

As she saw him run into the inferno, Lynne's heart turned over. "Oh, Jason," she whispered, knowing in a moment of horrible clarity that if he died, part of her would die, too.

Over the crackle of the flames she heard his voice shouting, "There's no exit at this end. We'll have to come back through the fire."

172

She held her breath. Another moment and he came hurtling through the wall of fire, shielding Tonio, swathed in the wet towels, in his arms. Together they ran back to the central part of the hall where the smoke was not so thick.

Lynne screamed. The shoulder of Jason's coat was on fire. She grabbed one of the wet towels from around Tonio and smothered the smoldering blaze.

Jason leaned against the wall in a spasm of coughing. She took Tonio from him and he motioned her down the stairs.

"Will you be all right?"

He nodded, again gesturing her to safety. Because of Tonio, she had to go down the stairs out the front door into the cool, life-giving freshness of the night.

The fire department had arrived. "There are people in the drawing room," she shouted in Italian. "They won't come out."

She laid Tonio on the grass. He was so white and still. She laid her ear to his chest and could feel that he was breathing.

Then Jason was kneeling beside her. He lifted the boy, cradling him in his arms. "Tonio!" he cried brokenly. "Speak to me, son. Tonio."

The child opened his eyes. "Zio Jason."

Jason buried his face in the boy's neck. "Oh, thank God. Thank God."

Lynne stared at the two of them. Jason had risked his life to save Tonio. She had seen anguish in his eyes as he had lifted the boy's still form, and the most exquisite relief when he saw that he was all right.

"Why, Jason," she said in wonder. "You love Tonio!"

CHAPTER FOURTEEN

At the emergency room of the hospital, the doctors had pronounced Tonio fit. They dressed the burn on Jason's shoulder, which was fortunately not a severe one.

The three of them started back to the hotel. Before they had left the villa, the fire department had had the blaze under control. The whole house would not be lost, only one wing badly damaged. The D'Allasios and their oddly assorted group of guests had been herded from the house and left roaming unconcernedly about the lawn.

"I told you we should have invited Nero to bring his fiddle," they heard Paola say as they got into Jason's car.

Lynne unlocked the door to their hotel suite and Jason carried Tonio inside. "He can sleep in the other twin bed in my room," Lynne said. "But first I think I'll bathe him and wash his singed hair. The smoke smell is so strong. Maybe he could sleep in one of your undershirts."

"I'll bring one in," Jason said.

He came back with the shirt and helped Lynne bathe, shampoo, and dry the tired child. The undershirt was miles too big, but Lynne found a long blue and white scarf to use as a sash and Jason stood him up on her dresser so that he could see himself in the mirror.

"Tell him I said that he looks so handsome he'll set a new fashion."

When she had repeated it, they were rewarded with the sound of a small giggle. Lynne tucked him up in bed and could see that he was almost asleep from exhaustion.

Jason knelt by his bed and kissed him, saying softly, "You belong to me now, old son. We belong to each other. I'll never leave you again."

Tonio couldn't understand the words, but from the look he gave his uncle, it seemed to Lynne that he had caught their meaning.

As Jason stood up and turned to her, she swayed and leaned against the door. One arm came out quickly to steady her. "What is it? Are you ill?"

She blinked. "No, I just went a little giddy. You know, I believe I haven't had anything to eat since breakfast."

"I'll order up an omelet. Meanwhile, why don't you have a bath too."

She stood under the shower a long time, and the water seemed to revive her. She toweled her hair damp dry and then got into her old cotton pajamas and the conservative brown robe.

She could hear the clink of the dishes as the waiter rolled the serving cart into the sitting room. She didn't wait to be summoned but went in directly. There was a delicious aroma of butter and mushrooms in the air. Without even waiting for Jason to seat her, she pulled a chair up to the table and whisked the domed cover off her plate.

"I must be absolutely famished," she said, "because right now that omelet looks more beautiful than anything I saw at the Uffizi Gallery. I wouldn't even trade it for a Botticelli."

Jason laughed and poured two glasses of white wine. She practically fell upon the huge basket of Italian bread. When she had finished the omelet,

Jason put several generous wedges of cheese on her plate and she helped herself to more bread and butter. She could feel life flowing back into her.

She poured out the coffee. "Are you finished. You don't want that last slice of fontina?"

They didn't speak until they had drunk their coffee. Then he handed her a brandy snifter and motioned her to an armchair.

"We have some talking to do, Lynne."

Obediently she sat where he had directed and took a sip of the brandy. Yes, she supposed they must talk.

"You said something very odd back at the villa, Lynne. You said, 'Jason, you love Tonio,' and you said it as if it was the biggest surprise of your life."

"Yes," she said slowly. "I guess it was."

"How could that surprise you when I've been working all this time in order to get custody and make him mine?"

"Justine said it was for the money."

"Justine! And what money are you talking about?"

"This morning—heavens, it seems like a year ago—she followed me from the hotel and caught me up and said she had to talk to me. Among other things, she said the whole plan was because of Tonio's inheritance—the half of the company that had belonged to his father. She said you wanted to be able to do as you liked with the firm without having to answer to anyone and that if anything should happen to Tonio—" She stopped, her eyes wide, and her hand flew to her mouth. "Oh, I'm sorry. I shouldn't be telling you this. It must be the wine."

"And you believed her!" he said bitterly.

"I wouldn't have believed it if one of your enemies said it, but she loves you. She's going to marry you."

"She loves a monster like me?"

Lynne twisted uncomfortably in her chair, but his

eyes compelled her to continue. "She said the quality of ruthlessness in you only made you more attractive to her because she knew how business operated."

The silence deepened and at last she said unhappily, "I wouldn't have taken her word for it but I asked Darren and he confirmed it."

"Darren said I only wanted Tonio's money!"

"He said it was true that Morgan had owned half the company and it now belonged to Tonio."

"That was all?"

She nodded. "Wasn't that enough?"

"A pity you didn't question him further. He could have told you that Tonio's inheritance is in trust—that I couldn't touch it or manipulate his holdings if I wanted to, that I'm answerable to the same trustees as when Morgan was alive and a partner though not active in the firm. They are three of the most reliable bankers in London and they'll keep their eagle eyes on Tonio's interests, just as they did on his father's before him."

"Oh, Jason, what can I say? Did Justine know that?"

"What do you think?"

She thought a minute, biting her lip. "Jason, I don't think you should be hurt by what she told me. It sounds very terrible, I know, but when you think about it, it just shows how much she loves you. She must have felt miserable knowing I was with you all this time. She must have felt so threatened that she was willing to say dreadful things in order to make me leave. It was foolish of her to be jealous, but I can understand how it could happen to a woman in love, so you mustn't feel she betrayed you. She was only trying to keep you. I'm sure of it."

He gave her a long, level look. "That's enormously comforting," he said dryly. "Did this great love of hers take into account how I'd feel about losing Tonio through her meddling?"

Lynne colored.

He shook his head. "Lynne, Lynne. You're the limit. Trying to protect my feelings by explaining away Justine's conniving on the grounds that she acted out of love. Do you really think I need a love like that? If you really think I'd fall apart at finding out what kind of woman Justine is, then all I can say is, you haven't been paying much attention the last few weeks."

She wasn't sure what he meant by that so she said nothing. She was still chagrined at having doubted him and also at having borne tales against Justine, but after the stress of the day the words had slipped out, and she didn't know how to set things right.

"The reasons I gave you for wanting Tonio were true ones," Jason said. "But there were two I left out. One seemed so self-evident that I didn't think I needed to say it. It's that I do love him. The other was something I hated to talk about because it seemed disloyal to my brother. I wanted to get Tonio away from his grandparents because I didn't trust them to bring up the boy. There's a wild streak in them—as you've now seen. They lead an unwholesome life—gambling, running with an unsavory set, even drugs. But there was nothing I could prove in a custody battle. I knew they'd be very circumspect if I brought suit until the matter was settled.

"There was a wild streak in Francesca too," he continued. "She seemed to bring out the recklessness in Morgan. She encouraged him to continue as a test driver long after he'd outgrown his boyish love of danger. But danger excited her. Morgan would have settled down soon, I know. Pray God if there's a reckless streak in Tonio I can guard him from coming to harm. But I don't believe in bad genes. I think it's the way a child is brought up that makes him what he is. For that reason, it seemed vital to get him away from his grandparents' influence before it was too late."

"I know it's too late for apologies," Lynne said, "but I wish I'd known. I might have been of more help. I could so easily have ruined everything for you, and I would have if the papers hadn't been signed in time."

"You have nothing to apologize for. I should have been more open with you. It was stiff-necked pride— not wanting to admit what kind of family my brother had married into. Until Justine spread her poison, you did everything you could to help. I couldn't have gotten anywhere without you."

The telephone shrilled and Lynne jumped.

"That must be Darren," Jason said guiltily. "I'd forgotten all about him. I promised to call the minute we got back with Tonio."

He picked up the receiver. "Yes, Darren. Everything's all right. No, we weren't out celebrating." His eyes met Lynne's and he grimaced. "It's a long story and I don't want to go into the details but there was a fire at the villa. We're all safe. Is Maddy with you? Yes, you can assure her we're all safe and Tonio's with us. And tell her she can take tomorrow morning off. Tell her it's a reward for always having my best interests at heart." His lips twisted slightly with amusement as he hung up.

"She's been so sweet to me," Lynne said.

His eyebrows rose in surprise. "Maddy? Sweet? She has a dozen good qualities, but sweet? You must have seen a very different side of her than the one I've seen."

"But she is. Oh, I'll admit she scared me to death

that first day. I'd never seen anyone so cool and efficient, as if she knew exactly what she was doing every minute and had no doubts about it being right. But then, just as she put me in the car to go out to Longridge, she gave me a package and said it was a personal present from her. It was some perfume. That was certainly a sweet thing to do. She must have known I was scared and wanted to give me a little token—for courage."

There was an odd glint in Jason's eyes. "As far back as that!"

"And before our—our trip." Her tongue stumbled over the word honeymoon. "She explained that we'd be having breakfast in our room and she didn't want me to be embarrassed by having to wear this brown robe because it wouldn't look as if I were really a bride, so she gave me that lovely blue and green one."

Jason threw back his head and laughed. "Well, I always felt she was one of the most farseeing people I ever knew. Remind me to take her to the races some time. She ought to be a whiz at picking winners."

She didn't understand him but said, "But doesn't that show she's sweet?"

"It shows, my innocent, that, as I said, she always has my best interests at heart."

"And she picked out those lovely clothes for me that first day. I don't think they were what she intended at first, but then I tried on that blue dinner dress, and all of a sudden everything changed and she said we'd take it—just like that—and all the other pretty things." She stared into the brandy snifter. "Though as it turned out, I think perhaps that was a mistake because if I had looked more dowdy when she met me, Justine might not have been so upset over our make-believe marriage. Don't you think that's possible?"

He didn't answer but raised his glass. "Madelaine Cheney, wherever you are, here's to your health. I salute you!"

"I truly didn't mean to cause trouble between you and Justine," Lynne said.

"Look, it's time for me to talk about Justine," he said.

"No, I don't want to hear it. That's a personal part of your life."

"You're going to listen." There was a note in his voice that would not be denied, and the old resentment of his authority flared in her, but she subsided.

"I knew Justine years ago when we were both very young," he said. "We had quite a romantic fling. I wasn't ready to settle down then. The business was my first priority at the time, my father having left it to Morgan and me not long before. Anyway, Justine chose Gerald Grant and we went our separate ways. I never saw her after that except casually at some big party, or I might run into them at the theatre. I had nothing to do with the break-up of their marriage.

"But eventually she and Grant separated and somehow our paths crossed again. By this time I knew there was something missing in my life. I'd devoted myself almost entirely to the business, but I looked at Morgan and, in spite of the instability of his life, I envied him Tonio. It seemed the right time to think about a family of my own.

"And there was Justine. What we had had in the early years was a romance, not a love affair, but I suppose one never quite forgets the object of one's early romantic fantasies. She had lived the same sort of life as I did; we knew many of the same people. And of course she was devilishly beautiful.

"There wasn't a formal engagement—she wasn't legally free. There was just an understanding that someday, when she was free, I'd be there.

"I think the first time I ever looked past that beautiful face was when I explained to her the need to get custody of Tonio—without waiting a year. She didn't take it well."

Something in his tone made Lynne understand that that was an understatement.

"Actually if she hadn't been so determined to fight Grant on every last point, their divorce could have been settled without too much trouble. But she wouldn't make any concessions. It seemed to be a point of honor with her to make him sweat for everything he could salvage from the years of work he'd put into the business.

"But she wanted it both ways. She wanted her pound of flesh from Grant but she wanted me to wait. She tried to forbid me to take the action I had decided on, but as you have pointed out"—he gave a small, wry smile—"I'm not accustomed to taking orders. So I said I'd do what I had to do, and she came around, or so I thought.

"I won't say I wasn't disappointed, but I tried to see it from her viewpoint. I hadn't expected her to be happy with the situation, but I did expect her to understand that it was necessary. I had explained to her what kind of life the D'Allasios led and why it was important to get Tonio away from them. And I expected that eventually, when all my problems and hers were settled, we'd get back to the point where we'd been before.

"There was one thing I hadn't counted on, though

—not being as farseeing as some of my associates."

He sat silent so long then, just looking at her, that she finally said, "What was that?"

"I think at first it was just having fun—perhaps for the first time in my life, a vacation with no business involved, where I had to slow down and really look around me, see things through fresh eyes, eyes that showed so much, lighting up in wonder and delight and reflecting that delight back at me. It was being near someone with such integrity that she suffered pangs of guilt over a deception, even though she was convinced it was in a good cause; someone who felt guilt every time any money was spent on her, some-one who was totally undemanding, not only unde-manding of gifts, but of my attention as well. If I had time to be with her, fine—we'd enjoy things together. If I was busy, she'd entertain herself. She was such a whole person within herself that she never needed to be the center of attention. She was full of pleasant surprises and a very relaxing companion."

Lynne had begun to feel a warm flush of embar-rassment as he talked, and she realized he was speak-ing of her. He was getting on personal, and therefore dangerous, ground. It was balm to her heart to know that he had considered her a good companion, that he respected her, but his nearness was working its magic on her. She was too aware of his masculine strength to be able to sit there, exhausted as she was, and keep her defenses up so that he wouldn't guess she yearned for him.

But he went inexorably on. "Then somehow it all changed and she wasn't relaxing to be with any-more."

She stared at him in bewilderment.

"I began to have to fight with myself every moment in her presence. I'd made her such a firm promise, you see, about what sort of honeymoon this would be. And for a while I did well. I intended to do things the gentlemanly way, not to take advantage of the intimacy of the situation. I was going to wait until we were at home where she was no longer under pressure, almost at my mercy, so to speak. And then one night I did a terrible thing. She had had an up-setting evening and was in a vulnerable mood and I—I lost control and did what I'd barely been able to restrain myself from doing for some time. I tried to make love to her. How could she forgive me? How could I forgive myself? But she was so lovely, so de-sirable, that I lost my head. I tried to apologize, but she kept me at arm's length from then on, and I couldn't blame her. I was eaten up with remorse and despair because I thought that if I'd ever had a chance with her, I'd ruined it all."

Tears were streaming down Lynne's face. "Jason, I think I'm dreaming. You can't mean what you're saying."

"What I mean, my darling, is that I adore you. I want to marry you. I love you."

"Oh, Jason, that night you pushed me away from you, I wanted to die. I thought you'd only kissed me because I'd nearly thrown myself at you and, well, you're a very masculine man and you just automatically responded. But you seemed so distressed afterward. I thought you were disgusted at having made love to a—to a nobody from the typing pool."

He groaned. "Oh, my darling girl. You're the most wonderful somebody I've ever known. But you've been driving me crazy. I wanted you so much I couldn't think straight, and you just shoved me farther and farther away."

"I was so afraid you'd see that—that I'd fallen in love with you," she said shyly. "I thought I could bear living without you, just with the memories, because I'd have to, you see, but I couldn't bear to have you pity me."

He came and knelt beside her, laying his head against her breast. She knew he could hear the wild, welcoming beating of her heart, but she only pressed him closer.

"Lynne," he whispered, "we're married legally. Would you—please—now—marry me for real? And forever?"

For an answer, she tipped up his face and bent her lips to his. As their mouths met, her own passion surged up to meet his, and they clung together, mindless of time.

At last he rose and took her hand. Then he stopped. "I've already said, 'With this ring I thee wed,' but I want to give you something more than the ring now—as a pledge of love." He reached into the pocket of his robe and took out a small package.

She opened it and there lay the golden face of the sun that she had admired in the jeweler's window on the Ponte Vecchio.

"I gathered from a pantomime of Tonio's in front of the shop window that you had liked it," he said. "I hope I understood him correctly."

She lifted it out of its box by the delicate chain. "Jason!" she cried, happiness spilling out of her eyes—not for the gold, but for the golden knowledge that it was she and no one else for whom he'd been buying a gift that day on the bridge. He'd been thinking of her!

"Put it on me," she said.

He took it out of her hand and laid it on the table. "Not now, love."

He lifted her in his arms with an easy strength that sent waves of excitement flooding through her as he started for his bedroom door. Then, remembering that under the dull brown robe she was wearing her plain cotton pajamas, she wailed, "Jason, it's our wedding night. I should be wearing my beautiful chiffon gown!"

He laughed. "My idiotic darling, don't you know that in another minute it won't make a bit of difference?"

She discovered he was right.

Love—the way you want it!

Candlelight Romances

INTRODUCING...

The Romance Magazine For The 1980's

Each exciting issue contains a full-length romance novel — the kind of first-love story we all dream about...

PLUS

other wonderful features such as a travelogue to the world's most romantic spots, advice about your romantic problems, a quiz to find the ideal mate for you and much, much more.

ROMANTIQUE: A complete novel of romance, plus a whole world of romantic features.

ROMANTIQUE: Wherever magazines are sold. Or write Romantique Magazine, Dept. C-1, 41 East 42nd Street, New York, N.Y. 10017

Once you've tasted joy and passion, do you dare dream of

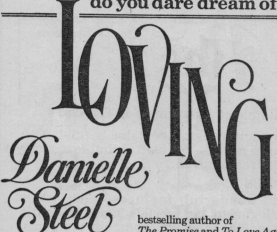

LOVING

Danielle Steel

bestselling author of
The Promise and *To Love Again*

Bettina Daniels lived in a gilded world—pampered, adored, adoring. She had youth, beauty and a glamorous life that circled the globe—everything her father's love, fame and money could buy. Suddenly, Justin Daniels was gone. Bettina stood alone before a mountain of debts and a world of strangers—men who promised her many things, who tempted her with words of love. But Bettina had to live her own life, seize her own dreams and take her own chances. But could she pay the bittersweet price?

A Dell Book ══════════════════ $2.75 (14684-4)

The first novel in the spectacular new
Heiress series

The English Heiress

Roberta Gellis

Leonie De Conyers—beautiful, aristocratic, she lived in the
shadow of the guillotine, stripped of everything she held
dear. Roger St. Eyre—an English nobleman, he set out to save
Leonie in a world gone mad.

They would be kidnapped, denounced and brutally separated. Driven by passion, they would escape France, return
to England, fulfill their glorious destiny and seize a lofty
dream.

A Dell Book $2.50 (12141-8)